A BETTER WORLD, BY JOVE!

They shut off winter soon after that. The heat trap was turned on full force; the skies cleared and it was lovely.

The first view I got of the Ganymede sky was a little after dawn next Sun phase. The heat trap made the sky a pale green—but Jupiter shone right through it, ruddy, orange, and *big*. Big and beautiful—I've never gotten tired of looking at Jupiter.

It hangs there in the sky, never rising, never setting . . . and you wonder what holds it up!

"Heinlein is more responsible for the development of modern science fiction than any other man!"

—*The New Yorker*

Farmer in the Sky

Robert A. Heinlein

A Del Rey Book

BALLANTINE BOOKS • NEW YORK

FOR SANDY

A Del Rey Book
Published by Ballantine Books

A condensed version was published in *Boy's Life Magazine* under
the title *Satellite Scout.*

ISBN 0-345-27596-9

This edition published by arrangement with Charles Scribner's
Sons

Manufactured in the United States of America

First Ballantine Books Edition: April 1975
Seventh Printing: October 1978

Contents

1. Earth

Our troop had been up in the High Sierras that day and we were late getting back. We had taken off from the camp field on time but Traffic Control swung us 'way east to avoid some weather. I didn't like it; Dad usually won't eat if I'm not home.

Besides that, I had had a new boy shoved off on me as co-pilot; my usual co-pilot and assistant patrol leader was sick, so our Scoutmaster, Mr. Kinski, gave me this twerp. Mr. Kinski rode in the other copter with the Cougar Patrol.

"Why don't you put on some speed?" the twerp wanted to know.

"Ever hear of traffic regulations?" I asked him.

The copter was on slave-automatic, controlled from the ground, and was cruising slowly, down a freight lane they had stuck us in.

The twerp laughed. "You can always have an emergency. Here—I'll show you." He switched on the mike. "Dog Fox Eight Three, calling traffic——"

I switched it off, then switched on again when Traffic answered and told them that we had called by mistake. The twerp looked disgusted. "Mother's good little boy!" he said in sticky sweet tones.

That was just the wrong thing to say to me. "Go

aft," I told him, "and tell Slats Keifer to come up here."

"Why? He's not a pilot."

"Neither are you, for my money. But he weighs what you do and I want to keep the crate trimmed."

He settled back in his seat. "Old Man Kinski assigned me as co-pilot; here I stay."

I counted to ten and let it ride. The pilot compartment of a ship in the air is no place for a fight. We had nothing more to say to each other until I put her down on North Diego Platform and cut the tip jets.

I was last one out, of course. Mr. Kinski was waiting there for us but I didn't see him; all I saw was the twerp. I grabbed him by the shoulder. "Want to repeat that crack now?" I asked him.

Mr. Kinski popped up out of nowhere, stepped between us and said, "Bill! Bill! What's the meaning of this?"

"I—" I started to say that I was going to slap the twerp loose from his teeth, but I thought better of it.

Mr. Kinski turned to the twerp. "What happened, Jones?"

"I didn't do anything! Ask anybody."

I was about to say that he could tell that to the Pilots' Board. Insubordination in the air is a serious matter. But that "Ask anybody" stopped me. Nobody else had seen or heard anything.

Mr. Kinski looked at each of us, then said, "Muster your patrol and dismiss them, Bill." So I did and went on home.

All in all, I was tired and jumpy by the time I got home. I had listened to the news on the way home; it wasn't good. The ration had been cut another ten calories—which made me still hungrier and reminded me that I hadn't been home to get Dad's supper. The newscaster went on to say that the Spaceship *Mayflower* had finally been commissioned and that the rolls were now opened for emigrants. Pretty lucky for them, I thought. No short rations. No twerps like Jones

And a brand new planet.

George—my father, that is—was sitting in the apartment, looking over some papers. "Howdy, George," I said to him, "eaten yet?"

"Hello, Bill. No."

"I'll have supper ready right away." I went into the pantry and could see that he hadn't eaten lunch, either. I decided to fix him a plus meal.

I grabbed two Syntho-Steaks out of the freezer and slapped them in quickthaw, added a big Idaho baked potato for Dad and a smaller one for me, then dug out a package of salad and let it warm naturally.

By the time I had poured boiling water over two soup cubes and over coffee powder the steaks were ready for the broiler. I transferred them, letting it cycle at medium rare, and stepped up the gain on the quickthaw so that the spuds would be ready when the steaks were—then back to the freezer for a couple of icekreem cake slices for dessert.

The spuds were ready. I took a quick look at my ration accounts, decided we could afford it, and set out a couple of pats of butterine for them. The broiler was ringing; I removed the steaks, set everything out, and switched on the candles, just as Anne would have done.

"Come and get it!" I yelled and turned back to enter the calorie and point score on each item from the wrappers, then shoved the wrappers in the incinerator. That way you never get your accounts fouled up.

Dad sat down as I finished. Elapsed time from scratch, two minutes and twenty seconds—there's nothing hard about cooking; I don't see why women make such a fuss about it. No system, probably.

Dad sniffed the steaks and grinned. "Oh boy! Bill, you'll bankrupt us."

"You let me worry," I said. "I'm still plus for this quarter." Then I frowned. "But I won't be, next quarter, unless they quit cutting the ration."

Dad stopped with a piece of steak on its way to his mouth. "Again?"

"Again. Look, George, I don't get it. This was a good crop year and they started operating the Montana yeast plant besides."

"You follow all the commissary news, don't you, Bill?"

"Naturally."

"Did you notice the results of the Chinese census as well? Try it on your slide rule."

I knew what he meant—and the steak suddenly tasted like old rubber. What's the use in being careful if somebody on the other side of the globe is going to spoil your try? "Those darned Chinese ought to quit raising babies and start raising food!"

"Share and share alike, Bill."

"But—" I shut up. George was right, he usually is, but somehow it didn't seem fair. "Did you hear about the *Mayflower?*" I asked to change the subject.

"What about the *Mayflower?*" Dad's voice was suddenly cautious, which surprised me. Since Anne died —Anne was my mother—George and I have been about as close as two people can be.

"Why, she was commissioned, that's all. They've started picking emigrants."

"So?" There was that cautious tone again. "What did you do today?"

"Nothing much. We hiked about five miles north of camp and Mr. Kinski put some of the kids through tests. I saw a mountain lion."

"Really? I thought they were all gone."

"Well, I thought I saw one."

"Then you probably did. What else?"

I hesitated, then told him about this twerp Jones. "He's not even a member of our troop. How does he get that way, interfering with my piloting?"

"You did right, Bill. Sounds as if this twerp Jones, as you call him, was too young to be trusted with a pilot's license."

"Matter of fact, he's a year older than I am."

"In my day you had to be sixteen before you could even go up for your license."

"Times change, George."

"So they do. So they do."

Dad suddenly looked sad and I knew he was thinking about Anne. I hastily said, "Old enough or not, how does an insect like Jones get by the temperament-stability test?"

"Psycho tests aren't perfect, Bill. Neither are people." Dad sat back and lit his pipe. "Want me to clean up tonight?"

"No, thanks." He always asked; I always turned him down. Dad is absent-minded; he lets ration points get into the incinerator. When I salvage, I really salvage. "Feel like a game of cribbage?"

"I'll beat the pants off you."

"You and who else?" I salvaged the garbage, burned the dishes, followed him into the living room. He was getting out the board and cards.

His mind wasn't really on the game. I was around the corner and ready to peg out before he was really under way. Finally he put down his cards and looked square at me. "Son——"

"Huh? I mean, 'Yes, George?' "

"I've decided to emigrate in the *Mayflower*."

I knocked over the cribbage board. I picked it up, eased my throttle, and tried to fly right. "That's swell! When do we leave?"

Dad puffed furiously on his pipe. "That's the point, Bill. You're not going."

I couldn't say anything. Dad had never done anything like this to me before. I sat there, working my mouth like a fish. Finally I managed, "Dad, you're joking."

"No, I'm not, Son."

"But why? Answer me that one question: why?"

"Now see here, Son——"

"Call me 'Bill'."

"Okay, Bill. It's one thing for me to decide to take my chances with colonial life but I've got no right to get *you* off to a bad start. You've got to finish your education. There are no decent schools on Ganymede. You get your education, then when you're grown, if you want to emigrate, that's your business."

"That's the reason? That's the *only* reason? To go to *school?*"

"Yes. You stay here and take your degree. I'd like to see you take your doctor's degree as well. Then, if you want to, you can join me. You won't have missed your chance; applicants with close relatives there have priority."

"No!"

Dad looked stubborn.

So did I, I guess. "George, I'm telling you, if you leave me behind, it won't do any good. I won't go to school. I can pass the exams for third class citizenship right now. Then I can get a work permit and——"

He cut me short. "You won't need a work permit. I'm leaving you well provided for, Bill. You'll——"

" 'Well provided for'! Do you think I'd touch a credit of yours if you go away and leave me? I'll live on my student's allowance until I pass the exams and get my work card."

"Bring your voice down, Son!" He went on, "You're proud of being a Scout, aren't you?"

"Well—yes."

"I seem to remember that Scouts are supposed to be obedient. And courteous, too."

That one was pretty hot over the plate. I had to think about it. "George——"

"Yes, Bill?"

"If I was rude, I'm sorry. But the Scout Law wasn't thought up to make it easy to push a Scout around. As long as I'm living in your home I'll do what you say. But if you walk out on me, you don't have any more claim on me. Isn't that fair?"

"Be reasonable, Son. I'm doing it for your own good."

"Don't change the subject, George. Is that fair or isn't it? If you go hundreds of millions of miles away, how can you expect to run my life after you're gone? I'll be on my own."

"I'll still be your father."

"Fathers and sons should stick together. As I recall, the fathers that came over in the original *Mayflower* brought their kids with them."

"This is different."

"How?"

"It's further, incredibly further—and dangerous."

"So was that move dangerous—half the Plymouth Rock colony died the first winter; everybody knows that. And distance doesn't mean anything; what matters is how long it takes. If I had had to walk back this afternoon, I'd still be hiking next month. It took the Pilgrims sixty-three days to cross the Atlantic or so they taught me in school—but this afternoon the caster said that the *Mayflower*—will reach Ganymede in sixty days. That makes Ganymede closer than London was to Plymouth Rock."

Dad stood up and knocked out his pipe. "I'm not going to argue, Son."

"And I'm not, either." I took a deep breath. I shouldn't have said the next thing I did say, but I was mad. I'd never been treated this way before and I guess I wanted to hurt back. "But I can tell you this: you're not the only one who is sick of short rations. If you think I'm going to stay here while you're eating high on the hog out in the colonies, then you had better think about it again. *I* thought we were partners."

That last was the meanest part of it and I should have been ashamed. That was what he had said to me the day after Anne died, and that was the way it had always been.

The minute I said it I knew why George had to emigrate and I knew it didn't have anything to do with ration points. But I didn't know how to unsay it.

Dad stared. Then he said slowly, "You think that's how it is? That I want to go away so I can quit skipping lunch to save ration points?"

"What else?" I answered. I was stuck in a groove; I didn't know what to say.

"Hmm . . . well, if you believe that, Bill, there is nothing I can say. I think I'll turn in."

I went to my room, feeling all mixed up inside. I wanted Mother around so bad I could taste it and I knew that George felt the same way. She would never have let us reach the point where we were actually shouting at each other—at least I had shouted. Besides that, the partnership was busted up, it would never be the same.

I felt better after a shower and a long massage. I knew that the partnership couldn't really be busted up. In the long run, when George saw that I had to go, he wouldn't let college stand in the way. I was sure of that—well, pretty sure at least.

I began to think about Ganymede.

Ganymede!

Why, I had never even been out to the Moon!

There was a boy in my class who had been born on the Moon. His parents were still there; he had been sent home for schooling. He gave himself airs as a deep-space man. But Luna was less than a quarter of a million miles away; you could practically throw rocks at it. It wasn't self-supporting; Moon Colony had the same rations as Earth. It was really part of Earth. But *Ganymede!*

Let's see—Jupiter was half a billion miles away, more or less, depending on the time of year. What was the tiny distance to the Moon compared with a jump like that?

Suddenly I couldn't remember whether Ganymede was Jupiter's third moon or fourth. And I just had to know. There was a book out in the living room that would tell and more besides—Ellsworth Smith's *A Tour of Earth's Colonies*. I went out to get it.

Dad hadn't gone to bed. He was sitting up, reading. I said, "Oh—hello," and went to look for the book. He nodded and went on reading.

The book wasn't where it should have been. I looked around and Dad said, "What are you looking for, Bill?"

Then I saw that he was reading it. I said, "Oh, nothing. I didn't know you were using it."

"This?" He held it up.

"It doesn't matter. I'll find something else."

"Take it. I'm through with it."

"Well . . . All right—thanks." I took it and turned away.

"Just a minute, Bill."

I waited. "I've come to a decision, Bill. I'm not going."

"*Huh?*"

"You were right about us being partners. My place is here."

"Yes, but— Look, George, I'm sorry I said what I did about rations. I know that's not the reason. The reason is—well, you've *got* to go." I wanted to tell him I knew the reason was Anne, but if I said Anne's name out loud I was afraid I'd bawl.

"You mean that you are willing to stay behind—and go to school?"

"Uh—" I wasn't quite ready to say that; I was dead set on going myself. "I didn't quite mean that. I meant that I know why you want to go, why you've *got* to go."

"Hmm . . ." He lit his pipe, making a long business of it. "I see. Or maybe I don't." Then he added, "Let's put it this way, Bill. The partnership stands. Either we both go, or we both stay—unless you decide of your own volition that you will stay to get your degree and join me out there later. Is that fair?"

"Huh? Oh, yes!"

"So let's talk about it later."

I said goodnight and ducked into my room quick. William, my boy, I told myself, it's practically in the bag—if you can just keep from getting soft-hearted and agreeing to a split up. I crawled into bed and opened the book.

Ganymede was Jupiter-III; I should have remembered that. It was bigger than Mercury, much bigger than the Moon, a respectable planet, even if it was a moon. The surface gravity was one third of Earth-normal; I would weigh about forty-five pounds there. First contacted in 1985—which I knew—and its atmosphere project started in 1998 and had been running ever since.

There was a stereo in the book of Jupiter as seen from Ganymede—round as an apple, ruddy orange, and squashed on both poles. And big as all outdoors. Beautiful. I fell asleep staring at it.

Dad and I didn't get a chance to talk for the next three days as my geography class spent that time in Antarctica. I came back with a frostbitten nose and some swell pix of penguins—and some revised ideas. I had had time to think.

Dad had fouled up the account book as usual but he had remembered to save the wrappers and it didn't take me long to straighten things out. After dinner I let him beat me two games, then said, "Look, George——"

"Yes?"

"You know what we were talking about?"

"Well, yes."

"It's this way. I'm under age; I can't go if you won't let me. Seems to me you ought to, but if you don't, I won't quit school. In any case, you ought to go—you *need* to go—you know why. I'm asking you to think it over and take me along, but I'm not going to be a baby about it."

Dad almost looked embarrassed. "That's quite a speech, Son. You mean you're willing to let me go, you stay here and go to school, and not make a fuss about it?"

"Well, not 'willing'—but I'd put up with it."

"Thanks." Dad fumbled in his pouch and pulled out a flat photo. "Take a look at this."

"What is it?"

"Your file copy of your application for emigration. I submitted it two days ago."

2. The Green-Eyed Monster

I wasn't much good in school for the next few days. Dad cautioned me not to get worked up over it; they hadn't approved our applications as yet. "You know, Bill, ten times as many people apply as can possibly go."

"But most of them want to go to Venus or Mars. Ganymede is too far away; that scares the sissies out."

"I wasn't talking about applications for all the colonies; I meant applications for Ganymede, specifically for this first trip of the *Mayflower*."

"Even so, you can't scare me. Only about one in ten can qualify. That's the way it's always been."

Dad agreed. He said that this was the first time in history that some effort was being made to select the best stock for colonization instead of using colonies as dumping grounds for misfits and criminals and failures. Then he added, "But look, Bill, what gives you the notion that you and I can necessarily qualify? Neither one of us is a superman."

That rocked me back on my heels. The idea that we might not be good enough hadn't occurred to me. "George, they couldn't turn us *down!*"

"They could and they might."

"But how? They need engineers out there and

you're tops. Me—I'm not a genius but I do all right in school. We're both healthy and we don't have any bad mutations; we aren't color blind or bleeders or anything like that."

"No bad mutations *that we know of*," Dad answered. "However, I agree that we seem to have done a fair job in picking our grandparents. I wasn't thinking of anything as obvious as that."

"Well, what, then? What could they possibly get us on?"

He fiddled with his pipe the way he always does when he doesn't want to answer right away. "Bill, when I pick a steel alloy for a job, it's not enough to say, 'Well, it's a nice shiny piece of metal; let's use it.' No, I take into account a list of tests as long as your arm that tells me all about that alloy, what it's good for and just what I can expect it to do in the particular circumstances I intend to use it. Now if you had to pick people for a tough job of colonizing, what would you look for?"

"Uh . . . I don't know."

"Neither do I. I'm not a social psychometrician. But to say that they want healthy people with fair educations is like saying that I want steel rather than wood for a job. It doesn't tell what sort of steel. Or it might not be steel that was needed; it might be titanium alloy. So don't get your hopes too high."

"But—well, look, what can we *do* about it?"

"Nothing. If we don't get picked, then tell yourself that you are a darn good grade of steel and that it's no fault of yours that they wanted magnesium."

It was all very well to look at it that way, but it worried me. I didn't let it show at school, though. I had already let everybody know that we had put in for Ganymede; if we missed—well, it would be sort of embarrassing.

My best friend, Duck Miller, was all excited about it and was determined to go, too.

"But how can you?" I asked. "Do your folks want to go?"

"I already looked into that," Duck answered. "All I have to have is a grown person as a sponsor, a guardian. Now if you can tease your old man into signing for me, it's in the bag."

"But what will *your* father say?"

"He won't care. He's always telling me that when he was my age he was earning his own living. He says a boy should be self reliant. Now how about it? Will you speak to your old man about it—tonight?"

I said I would and I did. Dad didn't say anything for a moment, then he asked: "You really want Duck with you?"

"Sure I do. He's my best friend."

"What does his father say?"

"He hasn't asked him yet," and then I explained how Mr. Miller felt about it.

"So?" said Dad. "Then let's wait and see what Mr. Miller says."

"Well—look, George, does that mean that you'll sign for Duck if his father says it's okay?"

"I meant what I said, Bill. Let's wait. The problem may solve itself."

I said, "Oh well, maybe Mr. and Mrs. Miller will decide to put in for it, too, after Duck gets them stirred up."

Dad just cocked an eyebrow at me. "Mr. Miller has, shall we say, numerous business interests here. I think it would be easier to jack up one corner of Boulder Dam than to get him to give them up."

"You're giving up *your* business."

"Not my business, my professional practice. But I'm not giving up my profession; I'm taking it with me."

I saw Duck at school the next day and asked him what his father had said.

"Forget it," he told me. "The deal is off."

"Huh?"

'My old man says that nobody but an utter idiot

would even think of going out to Ganymede. He says that Earth is the only planet in the system fit to live on and that if the government wasn't loaded up with a bunch of starry-eyed dreamers we would quit pouring money down a rat hole trying to turn a bunch of bare rocks in the sky into green pastures. He says the whole enterprise is doomed."

"You didn't think so yesterday."

"That was before I got the straight dope. You know what? My old man is going to take me into partnership. Just as soon as I'm through college he's going to start breaking me into the management end. He says he didn't tell me before because he wanted me to learn self reliance and initiative, but he thought it was time I knew about it. What do you think of that?"

"Why, that's pretty nice, I suppose. But what's this about the 'enterprise being doomed'?"

" 'Nice', he calls it! Well, my old man says that it is an absolute impossibility to keep a permanent colony on Ganymede. It's a perilous toehold, artificially maintained—those were his exact words—and someday the gadgets will bust and the whole colony will be wiped out, every man jack, and then we will quit trying to go against nature."

We didn't talk any more then as we had to go to class. I told Dad about it that night. "What do you think, George?"

"Well, there is something in what he says——"

"Huh?"

"Don't jump the gun. If everything went sour on Ganymede at once and we didn't have the means to fix it, it would revert to the state we found it in. But that's not the whole answer. People have a funny habit of taking as 'natural' whatever they are used to—but there hasn't been any 'natural' environment, the way they mean it, since men climbed down out of trees. Bill, how many people are there in California?"

"Fifty-five, sixty million."

"Did you know that the first four colonies here starved to death? 'S truth! How is it that fifty-odd million can live here and not starve? Barring short rations, of course."

He answered it himself. "We've got four atomic power plants along the coast just to turn sea water into fresh water. We use every drop of the Colorado River and every foot of snow that falls on the Sierras. And we use a million other gadgets. If those gadgets went bad—say a really big earthquake knocked out all four atomic plants—the country would go back to desert. I doubt if we could evacuate that many people before most of them died from thirst. Yet I don't think Mr. Miller is lying awake nights worrying about it. He regards Southern California as a good 'natural' environment.

"Depend on it, Bill. Wherever Man has mass and energy to work with and enough savvy to know how to manipulate them, he can create any environment he needs."

I didn't see much of Duck after that. About then we got our preliminary notices to take tests for eligibility for the Ganymede colony and that had us pretty busy. Besides, Duck seemed different—or maybe it was me. I had the trip on my mind and he didn't want to talk about it. Or if he did, he'd make some crack that rubbed me the wrong way.

Dad wouldn't let me quit school while it was still uncertain as to whether or not we would qualify, but I was out a lot, taking tests. There was the usual physical examination, of course, with some added wrinkles. A g test, for example—I could take up to eight gravities before I blacked out, the test showed. And a test for low-pressure tolerance and hemorrhaging—they didn't want people who ran to red noses and varicose veins. There were lots more.

But we passed them. Then came the psycho tests which were a lot worse because you never knew what was expected of you and half the time you didn't even know you were being tested. It started off with hypno-analysis, which really puts a fellow at a disadvantage. How do you know what you've blabbed while they've got you asleep?

Once I sat around endlessly waiting for a psychiatrist to get around to seeing me. There were a couple of clerks there; when I came in one of them dug my medical and psycho record out of file and laid it on a desk. Then the other one, a red-headed guy with a permanent sneer, said, "Okay, Shorty, sit down on that bench and wait."

After quite a while the redhead picked up my folder and started to read it. Presently he snickered and turned to the other clerk and said, "Hey, Ned—get a load of this!"

The other one read what he was pointing to and seemed to think it was funny, too. I could see they were watching me and I pretended not to pay any attention.

The second clerk went back to his desk, but presently the redhead went over to him, carrying my folder, and read aloud to him, but in such a low voice that I couldn't catch many of the words. What I did catch made me squirm.

When he had finished the redhead looked right at me and laughed. I stood up and said, "What's so funny?"

He said, "None of your business, Shorty. Sit down."

I walked over and said, "Let me see that."

The second clerk stuffed it into a drawer of his desk. The redhead said, "Mamma's boy wants to see it, Ned. Why don't you give it to him?"

"He doesn't really want to see it," the other one said.

"No, I guess not." The redhead laughed again and added, "And to think he wants to be a big bold colonist."

The other one looked at me while chewing a thumb-nail and said, "I don't think that's so funny. They could take him along to cook."

This seemed to convulse the redhead. "I'll bet he looks cute in an apron."

A year earlier I would have poked him, even though he outweighed me and outreached me. That "Mamma's boy" remark made me forget all about wanting to go to Ganymede; I just wanted to wipe the silly smirk off his face.

But I didn't do anything. I don't know why; maybe it was from riding herd on that wild bunch of galoots, the Yucca Patrol—Mr. Kinski says that anybody who can't keep order without using his fists can't be a patrol leader under him.

Anyhow I just walked around the end of the desk and tried to open the drawer. It was locked. I looked at them; they were both grinning, but I wasn't. "I had an appointment for thirteen o'clock," I said. "Since the doctor isn't here, you can tell him I'll phone for another appointment." And I turned on my heel and left.

I went home and told George about it. He just said he hoped I hadn't hurt my chances.

I never did get another appointment. You know what? They weren't clerks at all; they were psycho-metricians and there was a camera and a mike on me the whole time.

Finally George and I got notices saying that we were qualified and had been posted for the *Mayflower*, "subject to compliance with all requirements."

That night I didn't worry about ration points; I really set us out a feast.

There was a booklet of the requirements mentioned. "Satisfy all debts"—that didn't worry me; aside from a half credit I owed Slats Keifer I didn't have any. "Post an appearance bond"—George would take care of that. "Conclude any action before any court of superior jurisdiction"—I had never been in court except the Court of Honor. There were a flock of other things, but George would handle them.

I found some fine print that worried me. "George," I said, "It says here that emigration is limited to families with children."

He looked up. "Well, aren't we such a family? If you don't mind being classified as a child."

"Oh. I suppose so. I thought it meant a married couple and kids."

"Don't give it a thought."

Privately I wondered if Dad knew what he was talking about.

We were busy with innoculations and blood typing and immunizations and I hardly got to school at all. When I wasn't being stuck or being bled, I was sick with the last thing they had done to me. Finally we had to have our whole medical history tattooed on us—identity number, Rh factor, blood type, coag time, diseases you had had, natural immunities and inoculations. The girls and the women usually had it done in invisible ink that showed up only under infra-red light, or else they put it on the soles of their feet.

They asked me where I wanted it, the soles of my feet? I said no, I don't want to be crippled up; I had too much to do. We compromised on putting it where I sit down and then I ate standing up for a couple of days. It seemed a good place, private anyhow. But I had to use a mirror to see it.

Time was getting short; we were supposed to be at Mojave Space Port on 26 June, just two weeks away. It was high time I was picking out what to take. The allowance was fifty-seven and six-tenths pounds per person and had not been announced until all our body weights had been taken.

The booklet had said, "Close your terrestrial affairs as if you were dying." That's easy to say. But when you die, you can't take it with you, while here we could—fifty-seven-odd pounds of it.

The question was: what fifty-seven pounds?

My silkworms I turned over to the school biology lab and the same for the snakes. Duck wanted my aquarium but I wouldn't let him; twice he's had fish and twice he's let them die. I split them between two fellows in the troop who already had fish. The birds I gave to Mrs. Fishbein on our deck. I didn't have a cat or a dog; George says ninety floors up is no place to keep junior citizens—that's what he calls them.

I was cleaning up the mess when George came in. "Well," he says, "first time I've been able to come into your room without a gas mask."

I skipped it; George talks like that. "I still don't know what to do," I said, pointing at the heap on my bed.

"Microfilmed everything you can?"

"Yes, everything but this picture." It was a cabinet stereo of Anne, weighing about a pound and nine ounces.

"Keep that, of course. Face it, Bill, you've got to travel light. We're pioneers."

"I don't know what to throw out."

I guess I looked glum for he said, "Quit feeling sorry for yourself. Me, I've got to give up *this*—and that's tough, believe me." He held out his pipe.

"Why?" I asked. "A pipe doesn't weigh much."

"Because they aren't raising tobacco on Ganymede and they aren't importing any."

"Oh. Look, George, I could just about make it if it weren't for my accordion. But it licks me."

"Hmm . . . Have you considered listing it as a cultural item?"

"Huh?"

"Read the fine print. Approved cultural items are not covered by the personal weight schedule. They are charged to the colony."

It had never occurred to me that I might have anything that would qualify. "They wouldn't let me get away with it, George!"

"Can't rule you out for trying. Don't be a defeatist."

So two days later I was up before the cultural and scientific board, trying to prove that I was an asset. I knocked out *Turkey in the Straw*, Nehru's *Opus 81*, and the introduction to Morgenstern's *Dawn of the 22nd Century*, as arranged for squeeze boxes. I gave them *The Green Hills of Earth* for an encore.

They asked me if I liked to play for other people and told me politely that I would be informed as to the decision of the board . . . and about a week later I got a letter directing me to turn my accordion over to the Supply Office, Hayward Field. I was in, I was a "cultural asset"!

Four days before blast-off Dad came home early—he had been closing his office—and asked me if we could have something special for dinner; we were having guests. I said I supposed so; my accounts showed that we would have rations to turn back.

He seemed embarrassed. "Son——"

"Huh? Yes, George?"

"You know that item in the rules about families?"

"Uh, yes."

"Well, you were right about it, but I was holding out on you and now I've got to confess. I'm getting married tomorrow."

There was a sort of roaring in my ears. Dad couldn't have surprised me more if he had slapped me.

I couldn't say anything. I just stood there, looking at him. Finally I managed to get out, "But, George, you can't do that!"

"Why not, Son?"

"How about Anne?"

"Anne is dead."

"But— But—" I couldn't say anything more; I ducked into my room and locked myself in. I lay on the bed, trying to think.

Presently I heard Dad trying the latch. Then he tapped on the door and said, "Bill?"

I didn't answer. After a while he went away. I lay there a while longer. I guess I bawled, but I wasn't bawling over the trouble with Dad. It seemed the way it did the day Anne died, when I couldn't get it through my head that I wouldn't ever see her again. Wouldn't ever see her smile at me again and hear her say, "Stand tall, Billy."

And I would stand tall and she would look proud and pat my arm.

How could George do it? How could he bring some other woman into Anne's home?

I got up and had a look at myself in the mirror and then went in and set my 'fresher for a needle shower and a hard massage. I felt better afterwards, except that I still had a sick feeling in my stomach. The 'fresher blew me off and dusted me and sighed to a stop. Through the sound it seemed to me I could hear Anne speaking to me, but that must have been in my head.

She was saying, "Stand tall, Son." I got dressed again and went out.

Dad was messing around with dinner and I do mean messing. He had burned his thumb on the shortwave, don't ask me how. I had to throw out what he had been fiddling with, all except the salad. I picked out more stuff and started them cycling. Neither of us said anything.

I set the table for three and Dad finally spoke. "Better set it for four, Bill. Molly has a daughter, you know."

I dropped a fork. "Molly? You mean Mrs. Kenyon?"

"Yes. Didn't I tell you? No, you didn't give me a chance to."

I knew her all right. She was Dad's draftsman. I knew her daughter, too—a twelve-year-old brat. Somehow, it being Mrs. Kenyon made it worse, indecent. Why, she had even come to Anne's Farewell and had had the nerve to cry.

I knew now why she had always been so chummy with me whenever I was down at Dad's office. She had had her eye on George.

I didn't say anything. What was there to say?

I said "How do you do?" politely when they came in, then went out and pretended to fiddle with dinner. Dinner was sort of odd. Dad and Mrs. Kenyon talked and I answered when spoken to. I didn't listen. I was still trying to figure out how he could do it. The brat spoke to me a couple of times but I soon put her in her place.

After dinner Dad said how about all of us going to a show? I begged off, saying that I still had sorting to do. They went.

I thought and thought about it. Any way I looked at it, it seemed like a bad deal.

At first I decided that I wouldn't go to Ganymede after all, not if they were going. Dad would forfeit my bond, but I would work hard and pay it back—I wasn't going to owe *them* anything!

Then I finally figured out why Dad was doing it and I felt some better, but not much. It was too high a price.

Dad got home late, by himself, and tapped on my door. It wasn't locked and he came in. "Well, Son?" he said.

" 'Well' what?"

"Bill, I know that this business comes as a surprise to you, but you'll get over it."

I laughed, though I didn't feel funny. Get over it! Maybe he could forget Anne, but I never would.

"In the meantime," he went on, "I want you to behave yourself. I suppose you know you were as rude as you could be without actually spitting in their faces?"

"Me rude?" I objected. "Didn't I fix dinner for them? Wasn't I polite?"

"You were as polite as a judge passing sentence. And as friendly. You needed a swift kick to make you remember your manners."

I guess I looked stubborn. George went on, "That's done; let's forget it. See here, Bill—in time you are going to see that this was a good idea. All I ask you to do is to behave yourself in the meantime. I don't ask you to fall on their necks; I do insist that you be your own normal, reasonably polite and friendly self. Will you try?"

"Uh, I suppose so." Then I went on with, "See here, Dad, why did you have to spring it on me as a surprise?"

He looked embarrassed. "That was a mistake. I suppose I did it because I knew you would raise Cain about it and I wanted to put it off."

"But I would have understood if you had only *told* me. I know why you want to marry her——"

"Eh?"

"I should have known when you mentioned that business about rules. You have to get married so that we can go to Ganymede——"

"*What?*"

I was startled. I said, "Huh? That's right, isn't it? You told me so yourself. You said——"

"I said nothing of the sort!" Dad stopped, took a deep breath, then went on slowly, "Bill, I suppose you possibly could have gathered that impression—though I am not flattered that you could have entertained it. Now I'll spell out the true situation: Molly and I are not getting married in order to emigrate. We are emigrating because we are getting married. You may be too young to understand it, but I love Molly and Molly loves me. If I wanted to stay here, she'd stay. Since I want to go, she wants to go. She's wise enough to understand that I need to make a complete break with my old background. Do you follow me?"

I said I guessed so.

"I'll say goodnight, then."

I answered, "Goodnight." He turned away, but I added, "George—" He stopped.

I blurted out. "You don't love Anne any more, do you?"

Dad turned white. He started back in and then

stopped. "Bill," he said slowly, "it has been some years since I've laid a hand on you—but this is the first time I ever wanted to give you a thrashing."

I thought he was going to do it. I waited and I had made up my mind that if he touched me he was going to get the surprise of his life. But he didn't come any nearer; he just closed the door between us.

After awhile I took another shower that I didn't need and went to bed. I must have lain there an hour or more, thinking that Dad had wanted to hit me and wishing that Anne were around to tell me what to do. Finally I switched on the dancing lights and stared at them until they knocked me out.

Neither one of us said anything until breakfast was over and neither of us ate much, either. Finally Dad said, "Bill, I want to beg your pardon for what I said last night. You hadn't done or said anything to justify raising a hand to you and I had no business thinking it or saying it."

I said, "Oh, that's all right." I thought about it and added, "I guess I shouldn't have said what I did."

"It was all right to say it. What makes me sad is that you could have thought it. Bill, I've never stopped loving Anne and I'll never love her any less."

"But you said—" I stopped and finished, "I just don't get it."

"I guess there is no reason to expect you to." George stood up. "Bill, the ceremony is at fifteen o'clock. Will you be dressed and ready about an hour before that time?"

I hesitated and said, "I won't be able to, George. I've got a pretty full day."

His face didn't have any expression at all and neither did his voice. He said, "I see," and left the room. A bit later he left the apartment. A while later I tried to call him at his office, but the autosecretary ground out the old stall about "Would you like to record a message?" I didn't. I figured that George would be home some time before fifteen hundred and I got dressed in my best. I even used some of Dad's beard cream.

He didn't show up. I tried the office again, and again, got the "Would-you-like-to-record-a-message?" routine. Then I braced myself and looked up the code on Mrs. Kenyon.

He wasn't there. Nobody was there.

The time crawled past and there was nothing I could do about it. After a while it was fifteen o'clock and I knew that my father was off somewhere getting married but I didn't know where. About fifteen-thirty I went out and went to a show.

When I got back the red light was shining on the phone. I dialed playback and it was Dad: "Bill I tried to reach you but you weren't in and I can't wait. Molly and I are leaving on a short trip. If you need to reach me, call Follow Up Service, Limited, in Chi-cago—we'll be somewhere in Canada. We'll be back Thursday night. Goodbye." That was the end of the recording.

Thursday night—blast-off was Friday morning.

3. Space Ship *Bifrost*

Dad called me from Mrs. Kenyon's—I mean from Molly's—apartment Thursday night. We were both polite but uneasy. I said yes, I was all ready and I hoped they had had a nice time. He said they had and would I come over and we would all leave from there in the morning.

I said I hadn't known what his plans were, so I had bought a ticket to Mojave port and had reserved a room at Hotel Lancaster. What did he want me to do?

He thought about it and said, "It looks like you can take care of yourself, Bill."

"Of course I can."

"All right. We'll see you at the port. Want to speak to Molly?"

"Uh, no, just tell her hello for me."

"Thanks, I will." He switched off.

I went to my room and got my kit—fifty-seven and fifty-nine hundredths pounds; I couldn't have added a clipped frog's hair. My room was bare, except for my Scout uniform. I couldn't afford to take it, but I hadn't thrown it away yet.

I picked it up, intending to take it to the incinerator, then stopped. At the physical exam I had been listed at one hundred thirty-one and two tenths pounds mass in the clothes I would wear for blast off.

But I hadn't eaten much the last few days.

I stepped into the 'fresher and onto the scales—one hundred twenty-nine and eight tenths. I picked up the uniform and stepped back on the scales—one hundred thirty-two and five tenths.

William, I said, you get no dinner, you get no breakfast, and you drink no water tomorrow morning. I bundled up my uniform and took it along.

The apartment was stripped. As a surprise for the next tenant I left in the freezer the stuff I had meant to eat for supper, then switched all the gadgets to zero except the freezer, and locked the door behind me. It felt funny; Anne and George and I had lived there as far back as I could remember.

I went down to subsurface, across town, and caught the In-Coast tube for Mojave. Twenty minutes later I was at Hotel Lancaster in the Mojave Desert.

I soon found out that the "room" I had reserved was a cot in the billiard room. I trotted down to find out what had happened.

I showed the room clerk the 'stat that said I had a room coming to me. He looked at it and said, "Young man, have you ever tried to bed down six thousand people at once?"

I said no, I hadn't.

"Then be glad you've got a cot. The room you reserved is occupied by a family with nine children."

I went.

The hotel was a madhouse. I couldn't have gotten anything to eat even if I hadn't promised myself not to eat; you couldn't get within twenty yards of the dining room. There were children underfoot everywhere and squalling brats galore. There were emigrant families squatting in the ball room. I looked them over and wondered how they had picked them; out of a grab bag?

Finally I went to bed. I was hungry and got hungrier. I began to wonder why I was going to all this trouble to hang on to a Scout uniform I obviously wasn't going to use.

If I had had my ration book I would have gotten up and stood in line at the dining room—but Dad and I had turned ours in. I still had some money and thought about trying to find a free-dealers; they say you can find them around a hotel. But Dad says that "free-dealer" is a fake word; they are black marketeers and no gentleman will buy from them.

Besides that I didn't have the slightest idea of how to go about finding one.

I got up and got a drink and went back to bed and went through the relaxing routine. Finally I got to sleep and dreamed about strawberry shortcake with real cream, the kind that comes from cows.

I woke up hungry but I suddenly remembered that this was it!—my last day on Earth. Then I was too excited to be hungry. I got up, put on my Scout uniform and my ship suit over it.

I thought we would go right on board. I was wrong.

First we had to assemble under awnings spread out in front of the hotel near the embarking tubes. It wasn't air conditioned outside, of course, but it was early and the desert wasn't really hot yet. I found the letter "L" and sat down under it, sitting on my baggage. Dad and his new family weren't around yet; I began to wonder if I was going to Ganymede by myself. I didn't much care.

Out past the gates about five miles away, you could see the ships standing on the field, the *Daedalus* and the *Icarus,* pulled off the Earth-Moon run for this one trip, and the old *Bifrost* that had been the shuttle rocket to Supra-New-York space station as far back as I could remember.

The *Daedalus* and the *Icarus* were bigger but I hoped I would get the *Bifrost;* she was the first ship I ever saw blast off.

A family put their baggage down by mine. The

mother looked out across the field and said, "Joseph, which one is the *Mayflower?*"

Her husband tried to explain to her, but she still was puzzled. I nearly burst, trying to keep from laughing. Here she was, all set to go to Ganymede and yet she was so dumb she didn't even know that the ship she was going in had been built out in space and couldn't land anywhere.

The place was getting crowded with emigrants and relatives coming to see them off, but I still didn't see anything of Dad. I heard my name called and turned around and there was Duck Miller. "Gee, Bill," he said, "I thought I'd missed you."

"Hi, Duck. No, I'm still here."

"I tried to call you last night but your phone answered 'service discontinued,' so I hooked school and came up."

"Aw, you shouldn't have done that."

"But I wanted to bring you this." He handed me a package, a whole pound of chocolates. I didn't know what to say.

I thanked him and then said, "Duck, I appreciate it, I really do. But I'll have to give them back to you."

"Huh? Why?"

"Weight. Mass, I mean. I can't get by with another ounce."

"You can carry it."

"That won't help. It counts just the same."

He thought about it and said, "Then let's open it."

I said, "Fine," and did so and offered him a piece. I looked at them myself and my stomach was practically sitting up and begging. I don't know when I've been so hungry.

I gave in and ate one. I figured I would sweat it off anyhow; it was getting hot and I had my Scout uniform on under my ship suit—and that's no way to dress for the Mojave Desert in June! Then I was thirstier than ever, of course; one thing leads to another.

I went over to a drinking fountain and took a very small drink. When I came back I closed the candy box and handed it back to Duck and told him to pass it around at next Scout meeting and tell the fellows I wished they were going along. He said he would and added, "You know, Bill, I wish I was going. I really do."

I said I wished he was, too, but when did he change his mind? He looked embarrassed but about then Mr. Kinski showed up and then Dad showed up, with Molly and the brat—Peggy—and Molly's sister, Mrs. van Metre. Everybody shook hands all around and Mrs. van Metre started to cry and the brat wanted to know what made my clothes so bunchy and what was I sweating about?

George was eyeing me, but about then our names were called and we started moving through the gate.

George and Molly and Peggy were weighed through and then it was my turn. My baggage was right on the nose, of course, and then I stepped on the scales. They read one hundred and thirty-one and one tenth pounds—I could have eaten another chocolate.

"Check!" said the weightmaster, then he looked up and said, "What in the world have you got on, son?"

The left sleeve of my uniform had started to unroll and was sticking out below the half sleeve of my ship suit. The merit badges were shining out like signal lights.

I didn't say anything. He started feeling the lumps the uniform sleeves made. "Boy," he said, "you're dressed like an arctic explorer; no wonder you're sweating. Didn't you know you weren't supposed to wear anything but the gear you were listed in?"

Dad came back and asked what the trouble was? I just stood there with my ears burning. The assistant weightmaster got into the huddle and they argued what should be done. The weightmaster phoned somebody and finally he said, "He's inside his weight limit;

if he wants to call that monkey suit part of his skin, we'll allow it. Next customer, please!"

I trailed along, feeling foolish. We went down inside and climbed on the slide strip, it was cool down there, thank goodness. A few minutes later we got off at the loading room down under the rocket ship. Sure enough, it was the *Bifrost*, as I found out when the loading elevator poked above ground and stopped at the passenger port. We filed in.

They had it all organized. Our baggage had been taken from us in the loading room; each passenger had a place assigned by his weight. That split us up again; I was on the deck immediately under the control room. I found my place, couch 14-D, then went to a view port where I could see the *Daedalus* and the *Icarus*.

A brisk little stewardess, about knee high to a grasshopper, checked my name off a list and offered me an injection against dropsickness. I said no, thanks.

She said, "You've been out before?"

I admitted I hadn't; she said, "Better take it."

I said I was a licensed air pilot; I wouldn't get sick. I didn't tell her that my license was just for copters. She shrugged and turned away. A loudspeaker said, "The *Daedalus* is cleared for blasting." I moved up to get a good view.

The *Daedalus* was about a quarter of a mile away and stood up higher than we did. She had fine lines and was a mighty pretty sight, gleaming in the morning sunshine. Beyond her and to the right, clear out at the edge of the field, a light shone green at the traffic control blockhouse.

She canted slowly over to the south, just a few degrees.

Fire burst out of her base, orange, and then blinding white. It splashed down into the ground baffles and curled back up through the ground vents. She lifted.

She hung there for a breath and you could see the hills shimmer through her jet. And she was gone.

Just like that—she was gone. She went up out of there like a scared bird, just a pencil of white fire in the sky, and was gone while we could still hear and feel the thunder of her jets inside the compartment.

My ears were ringing. I heard someone behind me say, "But I haven't had breakfast. The Captain will just have to wait. Tell him, Joseph."

It was the woman who hadn't known that the *Mayflower* was a space-to-space ship. Her husband tried to hush her up, but he didn't have any luck. She called over the stewardess. I heard her answer, "But, madam, you can't speak to the Captain now. He's preparing for blast-off."

Apparently that didn't make any difference. The stewardess finally got her quiet by solemnly promising that she could have breakfast after blast-off. I bent my ears at that and I decided to put in a bid for breakfast, too.

The *Icarus* took off twenty minutes later and then the speaker said, "All hands! Acceleration stations— prepare to blast off." I went back to my couch and the stewardess made sure that we were all strapped down. She cautioned us not to unstrap until she said we could. She went down to the deck below.

I felt my ears pop and there was a soft sighing in the ship. I swallowed and kept swallowing. I knew what they were doing: blowing the natural air out and replacing it with the standard helium-oxygen mix at half sea-level pressure. But the woman—the same one—didn't like it. She said, "Joseph, my head aches. Joseph, I can't breathe. Do something!"

Then she clawed at her straps and sat up. Her husband sat up, too, and forced her back down.

The *Bifrost* tilted over a little and the speaker said, "Minus three minutes!"

After a long time it said, "Minus two minutes!"

And then "Minus one minute!" and another voice took up the count:

"Fifty-nine! Fifty-eight! Fifty-seven!"

My heart started to pound so hard I could hardly hear it. But it went on: "—thirty-five! Thirty-four! Thirty-three! Thirty-two! Thirty-one! *Half!* Twenty-nine! Twenty-eight!"

And it got to be: "*Ten!*"

And "Nine!"

"Eight!

"Seven!

"And six!

"And five!

"And four!

"And three!

"And two——"

I never did hear them say "one" or "fire" or whatever they said. About then something fell on me and I thought I was licked. Once, exploring a cave with the fellows, a bank collapsed on me and I had to be dug out. It was like that—but nobody dug me out.

My chest hurt. My ribs seemed about to break. I couldn't lift a finger. I gulped and couldn't get my breath.

I wasn't scared, not really, because I knew we would take off with a high g, but I was awfully uncomfortable. I managed to turn my head a little and saw that the sky was already purple. While I watched, it turned black and the stars came out, millions of stars. And yet the Sun was still streaming in through the port.

The roar of the jets was unbelievable but the noise started to die out almost at once and soon you couldn't hear it at all. They say the old ships used to be noisy even after you passed the speed of sound; the *Bifrost* was not. It got as quiet as the inside of a bag of feathers.

There was nothing to do but lie there, stare out at

that black sky, try to breathe, and try not to think about the weight sitting on you.

And then, so suddenly that it made your stomach turn flip-flops, you didn't weigh anything at all.

4. Captain DeLongPre

Let me tell you that the first time you fall is no fun. Sure, you get over it. If you didn't you would starve. Old space hands even get so they like it—weightlessness, I mean. They say that two hours of weightless sleep is equal to a full night on Earth. I got used to it, but I never got to like it.

The *Bifrost* had blasted for a little more than three minutes. It seemed lots longer because of the high acceleration; we had blasted at nearly six g. Then she was in free orbit for better than three hours and we fell the whole time, until the Captain started to maneuver to match orbits with the *Mayflower*.

In other words we fell straight up for more than twenty thousand miles.

Put that way, it sounds silly. Everybody knows that things don't fall *up*; they fall *down*.

Everybody knew the world was flat, too.

We fell up.

Like everybody, I had had the elements of space ballistics in grammar school physics, and goodness knows there have been enough stories about how you float around in a spaceship when it's in a free orbit. But, take it from me, you don't really believe it until you've tried it.

Take Mrs. Tarbutton—the woman who wanted breakfast. I suppose she went to school like everybody else. But she kept insisting that the Captain had to do something about it. What he could do I don't know; find her a small asteroid, maybe.

Not that I didn't sympathize with her—or with myself, I guess. Ever been in an earthquake? You know how everything you ever depended on suddenly goes back on you and *terra firma* isn't *firma* any longer? It's like that, only much worse. This is no place to review grammar school physics but when a spaceship is in a free trajectory, straight up or any direction, the ship and everything in it moves along together and you *fall*, endlessly—and your stomach darn near falls out of you.

That was the first thing I noticed. I was strapped down so that I didn't float away, but I felt weak and shaky and dizzy and as if I had been kicked in the stomach. Then my mouth filled with saliva and I gulped and I was awfully sorry I had eaten that chocolate.

But it didn't come up, not quite.

The only thing that saved me was no breakfast. Some of the others were not so lucky. I tried not to look at them. I had intended to unstrap as soon as we went free and go to a port so I could look at Earth, but I lost interest in that project entirely. I stayed strapped down, and concentrated on being miserable.

The stewardess came floating out the hatch from the next deck, shoved herself along with a toe, checked herself with a hand at the center stanchion, and hovered in the air in a swan dive, looking us over. It was very pretty to watch if I'd been in shape to appreciate it.

"Is everybody comfy?" she said cheerfully.

It was a silly remark but I suppose nurses get that way. Somebody groaned and a baby on the other side of the compartment started to cry. The stewardess moved over to Mrs. Tarbutton and said, "You may have breakfast now. What would you like? Scrambled eggs?"

I clamped my jaw and turned my head away, wishing she would shut up. Then I looked back. She had paid for that silly remark—and she had to clean it up.

When she was through with Mrs. Tarbutton I said, "Uh—oh, Miss——"

"Andrews."

"Miss Andrews, could I change my mind about that drop-sick injection?"

"Righto, chum," she agreed, smiling, and whipped out an injector from a little kit she had at her belt. She gave me the shot. It burned and for a moment I thought I was going to lose the chocolate after all. But then things quieted down and I was almost happy in a miserable sort of way.

She left me and gave shots to some others who had kidded themselves the same way I had. Mrs. Tarbutton she gave another sort of shot to knock her out entirely. One or two of the hardier souls unstrapped themselves and went to the ports; I decided I was well enough to try it.

It's not as easy as it looks, this swimming around in free fall. I undid the safety belts and sat up; that's all I meant to do. Then I was scrambling in the air, out of control, trying frantically to grasp at anything.

I turned over in the air and cracked the back of my head against the underside of the control room deck and saw stars, not the ones out the ports—some of my own. Then the deck with the couches on it was approaching me slowly.

I managed to grab a safety belt and came to anchor. The couch it belonged to was occupied by a little plump man. I said, "Excuse me."

He said, "Don't mention it," and turned his face away, looking as if he hated me. I couldn't stay there and I couldn't even get back to my own couch without grabbing handholds on other couches that were occupied, too, so I pushed off again, very gently this time, and managed to grab hold when I bumped against the other deck.

It had handholds and grab lines all over it. I didn't let go again, but pulled myself along, monkey fashion, to one of the ports.

And there I got my first view of Earth from space.

I don't know what I expected, but it wasn't what I expected. There it was, looking just like it does in the geography books, or maybe more the way it does in the station announcements of Super-New-York TV station. And yet it was different. I guess I would say it was like the difference between being told about a good hard kick in the rear and actually being kicked.

Not a transcription. Alive.

For one thing it wasn't prettily centered in a television screen; it was shouldering into one side of the frame of the port, and the aft end of the ship cut a big chunk out of the Pacific Ocean. And it was moving, shrinking. While I hung there it shrunk to about half the size it was when I first got there and got rounder and rounder. Columbus was right.

From where I was it was turned sideways; the end of Siberia, then North America, and finally the north half of South America ran across from left to right. There were clouds over Canada and the eastern part of the rest of North America; they were the whitest white I ever saw—whiter than the north pole cap. Right opposite us was the reflection of the Sun on the ocean; it hurt my eyes. The rest of the ocean was almost purple where there weren't clouds.

It was so beautiful my throat ached and I wanted to reach out and touch it.

And back of it were stars, even brighter and bigger and more of them than the way they look from Little America.

Pretty soon there were more people crowding around, trying to see, and kids shoving and their mothers saying, "Now, now, darling!" and making silly remarks themselves. I gave up. I pulled myself back

to my couch and put one belt around me so I wouldn't
float away and thought about it. It makes you proud
to know that you come from a big, fancy planet like
that. I got to thinking that I hadn't seen all of it, not
by a long sight, in spite of all the geography trips I
had made and going to one Scout round-up in Switzer-
land and the time George and Anne and I went to
Siam.

And now I wasn't going to see any more of it. It
made me feel pretty solemn.

I looked up; there was a boy standing in front of
me. He said, "What's the trouble, William, my boy?
Dropsick?"

It was that twerp Jones. You could have knocked me
out with a feather. If I had known he was going to
emigrate, I would have thought twice about it.

I asked him where in the world he had come from.

"The same place you did, naturally. I asked you a
question."

I informed him that I was not dropsick and asked
him whatever gave him that silly notion. He reached
out and grabbed my arm and turned it so that the
red spot the injection had made showed. He laughed
and I jerked my arm away.

He laughed again and showed me his arm; it had
a red spot on it, too. "Happens to the best of us," he
said. "Don't be shy about it."

Then he said, "Come on. Let's look around the joint
before they make us strap down again."

I went along. He wasn't what I would pick for a
buddy but he was a familiar face. We worked our way
over to the hatch to the next deck. I started to go
through but Jones stopped me. "Let's go into the control room," he suggested.

"Huh? Oh, they wouldn't let us!"

"Is it a crime to try? Come on." We went back the
other way and through a short passage. It ended in a
door that was marked: CONTROL ROOM—STAY
OUT! Somebody had written under it: *This means*

you!!! and somebody else had added: *Who? Me?*

Jones tried it; it was locked. There was a button beside it; he pushed it.

It opened and we found ourselves staring into the face of a man with two stripes on his collar. Behind him was an older man with four stripes on his; he called out, "Who is it, Sam? Tell 'em we're not in the market."

The first man said, "What do you kids want?"

Jones said, "Please, sir, we're interested in astrogation. Could we have permission to visit the control room?"

I could see he was going to chuck us out and I had started to turn away when the older man called out, "Oh, shucks, Sam, bring 'em in!"

The younger fellow shrugged and said, "As you say, Skipper."

We went in and the Captain said, "Grab on to something; don't float around. And don't touch anything, or I'll cut your ears off. Now who are you?"

We told him; he said, "Glad to know you, Hank—same to you, Bill. Welcome aboard." Then he reached out and touched the sleeve of my uniform—it had come loose again. "Son, your underwear is showing."

I blushed and told him how I happened to be wearing it. He laughed and said, "So you swindled us into lifting it anyway. That's rich—eh, Sam? Have a cup of coffee."

They were eating sandwiches and drinking coffee—not from cups, of course, but from little plastic bags like they use for babies. The bags even had nipples on them. I said no, thanks. While the shot Miss Andrews gave me had made me feel better, it hadn't made me feel that much better. Hank Jones turned it down, too.

The control room didn't have a port in it of any sort. There was a big television screen forward on the bulkhead leading to the nose, but it wasn't turned on. I wondered what Mrs. Tarbutton would think if she knew that the Captain couldn't see where we were going and didn't seem to care.

I asked him about the ports. He said ports were strictly for tourists. "What would you do with a port if you had one?" he asked. "Stick your head out the window and look for road signs? We can see anything we need to see. Sam, heat up the video and show the kids."

"Aye aye, Skipper." The other chap swam over to his couch and started turning switches. He left his sandwich hanging in the air while he did so.

I looked around. The control room was circular and the end we came in was bigger than the other end; it was practically up in the nose of the ship and the sides sloped in. There were two couches, one for the pilot and one for the co-pilot, flat against the wall that separated the control room from the passenger compartments. Most of the space between the couches was taken up by the computer.

The couches were fancier than the ones the passengers had; they were shaped to the body and they lifted the knees and the head and back, like a hospital bed, and there were arm rests to support their hands over the ship's controls. An instrument board arched over each couch at the middle, where the man in the couch could see the dials and stuff even when his head was pushed back into the cushions by high g.

The TV screen lighted up and we could see Earth; it filled most of the screen. "That's 'View Aft'," the co-pilot said, "from a TV camera in the tail. We've got 'em pointing in all directions. Now we'll try 'View Forward'." He did, but it didn't amount to anything, just a few tiny little dots that might have been stars. Hank said you could see more stars out a port.

"You don't use it to look at stars," he answered. "When you need to take a star sight, you use the coelostats. Like this." He lay back on the couch and reached behind his head, pulling an eye piece arrangement over his face until the rubber guard fitted over one eye without lifting his head off the couch. "Coelostat" is just a trick name for a telescope with a periscope built into it. He didn't offer to let us look through it, so I looked back at the instrument board. It had a couple of radar presentations, much like you'll find in any atmosphere ship, even in a copter, and a lot of other instruments, most of which I didn't understand, though some of them were pretty obvious, like approach rate and throat temperature and mass ratio and ejection speed and such.

"Watch this," said the co-pilot. He did something at his controls; one of the tiny blips on the TV screen lit up very brightly, blinked a few times, then died away. "That was Supra-New-York; I triggered her radar beacon. You are not seeing it by television; it's radar brought on to the same screen." He fiddled with the controls again and another light blinked, two longs and a short. "That's where they're building the *Star Rover*."

"Where's the *Mayflower*?" Hank asked.

"Want to see where you're going, eh?" He touched his controls again; another light came on, way off to one side, flashing in groups of three.

I said it didn't look much like we were going there. The Captain spoke up. "We're taking the long way round, past the fair grounds. That's enough, Sam. Lock your board."

We all went back where the Captain was still eating. "You an Eagle Scout?" he asked me. I said yes and Hank said he was too.

"How old were you when you made it?" he wanted to know. I said I had been thirteen, so Hank said twelve, whereupon the Captain claimed he had made it at eleven. Personally I didn't believe either one of them.

The Captain said so now we were going out to Ganymede; he envied both of us. The co-pilot said what was there to envy about that?

The Captain said, "Sam, you've got no romance in your soul. You'll live and die running a ferry boat."

"Maybe so," the co-pilot answered, "but I sleep home a lot of nights."

The Captain said pilots should not marry. "Take me," he said, "I always wanted to be a deep-space man. I was all set for it, too, when I was captured by pirates and missed my chance. By the time I had the chance again, I was married."

"You and your pirates," said the co-pilot.

I kept my face straight. Adults always think anybody younger will swallow anything; I try not to disillusion them.

"Well, all that's as may be," said the Captain. "You two young gentlemen run along now. Mr. Mayes and I have got to fake up a few figures, or we'll be landing this bucket in South Brooklyn."

So we thanked him and left.

I found Dad and Molly and the Brat in the deck aft of my own. Dad said, "Where have you been, Bill? I've been looking all over the ship for you."

I told them, "Up in the control room with the Captain."

Dad looked surprised and the Brat made a face at me and said, "Smarty, you have not. Nobody can go up there."

I think girls should be raised in the bottom of a deep, dark sack until they are old enough to know better. Then when it came time, you could either let them out or close the sack and throw them away, whichever was the best idea.

Molly said, "Hush, Peggy."

I said, "You can just ask Hank. He was with me. We——" I looked around but Hank was gone. So I told them what had happened, all but the part about pirates.

When I finished the Brat said, "I want to go into the control room, too."

Dad said he didn't think it could be arranged. The Brat said, "Why not? Bill went."

Molly said hush again. "Bill is a boy and older than you are." The Brat said it wasn't fair.

I guess she had something there—but things hardly ever are. Dad went on, "You should feel flattered, Bill, being entertained by the famous Captain DeLongPre."

"Huh?"

"Maybe you are too young to remember it. He let himself be sealed into one of the robot freighters used to jump thorium ore from the lunar mines—and busted up a ring of hijackers, a gang the newscasters called the 'Ore Pirates.' "

I didn't say anything.

I wanted to see the *Mayflower* from space, but they made us strap down before I could locate it. I got a pretty good view of Supra-New-York though; the *Mayflower* was in the 24-hour orbit the space station rides in and we were closing almost directly on it when the word came to strap down.

Captain DeLongPre was quite some pilot. He didn't fiddle around with jockeying his ship into the new groove; he gave one long blast on the jet, the right time, the right amount, and the right direction. As it says in the physics book, "every one-plane correction-of-orbit problem which can be solved at all, can be solved with a single application of acceleration"—provided the pilot is good enough.

He was good enough. When we went weightless again, I looked over my shoulder out a port and there was the *Mayflower*, with the Sun gleaming on her, large as life and not very far away. There was the softest sort of a correction bump and the loudspeaker sang out, "Contact completed. You may unstrap."

I did and went to the port from which we could see the *Mayflower*. It was easy to see why she could never land; she had no airfoils of any sort, not even fins, and she was the wrong shape—almost spherical except that one side came out to a conical point.

She looked much too small—then I realized that a little bulge that was sticking out past her edge at one point was actually the bow of the *Icarus,* unloading on the far side. Then suddenly she was enormous and the little flies on her were men in space suits.

One of them shot something at us and a line came snaking across. Before the knob on the end of it quite reached us there was a bright purple brush discharge from the end of it and every hair on my head stood straight up and my skin prickled. A couple of the women in the compartment squealed and I heard Miss Andrews soothing them down and telling them that it was just the electrical potential adjusting between the two ships. If she had told them it was a bolt of lightning she would have been just as correct, but I don't suppose that would have soothed them.

I wasn't scared; any kid who had fooled around with radio or any sort of electronics would have expected it.

The knob on the line clunked against the side of the ship and after a bit the little line was followed by a heavier line and then they warped us together, slowly. The *Mayflower* came up until she filled the port.

After a bit my ears popped and the loudspeaker said, "All hands—prepare to disembark."

Miss Andrews made us wait quite a while, then it was our deck's turn and we pulled ourselves along to the deck we had come in by. Mrs. Tarbutton didn't come along; she and her husband were having some sort of a discussion with Miss Andrews.

We went right straight out of our ship, through a jointed steel drum about ten feet long, and into the *Mayflower.*

5. Captain Harkness

Do you know the worst thing about spaceships? They smell bad.

Even the *Mayflower* smelled bad and she was brand new. She smelled of oil and welding and solvents and dirty, sweaty smells of all the workmen who had lived in her so long. Then we came, three shiploads of us, most of us pretty whiff with that bad odor people get when they're scared or very nervous. My stomach still wasn't happy and it almost got me.

The worst of it is that there can't be very good 'freshers in a ship; a bath is a luxury. After the ship got organized we were issued tickets for two baths a week, but how far does that go, especially when a bath means two gallons of water to sponge yourself off with?

If you felt you just *had* to have a bath, you could ask around and maybe buy a ticket from somebody who was willing to skip one. There was one boy in my bunk room who sold his tickets for four weeks running until we all got sick of it and gave him an unscheduled bath with a very stiff brush. But I'm getting ahead of myself.

And you couldn't burn your clothes either; you had to *wash* them.

When we first got into the *Mayflower* it took them

maybe half an hour to get us all sorted out and into our acceleration couches. The people from the *Daedalus* and the *Icarus* were supposed to be stowed away by the time we got there, but they weren't and the passageways were traffic jams. A traffic jam when everybody is floating, and you don't know which end is up, is about eight times as confusing as an ordinary one.

There weren't any stewardesses to get us straight, either; there were emigrants instead, with signs on their chests reading SHIP'S AIDE—but a lot of them needed aid themselves; they were just as lost as anybody else. It was like amateur theatricals where the ushers don't know how to find the reserved seats.

By the time I was in the bunk room I was assigned to and strapped down there were bells ringing all over the place and loudspeakers shouting: "Prepare for acceleration! Ten minutes!"

Then we waited.

It seemed more like half an hour. Presently the count-off started. I said to myself, William, if the blast-off from Earth was rugged, this is going to knock the teeth right out of your head. I knew what we were going to build up to—better than ninety-three miles per second. That's a third of a million miles an hour! Frankly I was scared.

The seconds ticked away; there was a soft push that forced me down against the cushions—and that was all. I just lay there; the ceiling was the ceiling again and the floor was under me, but I didn't feel extra heavy, I felt fine.

I decided that was just the first step; the next one would be a dilly.

Up overhead in the bunk room was a display screen; it lighted up and I was looking into the face of a man with four collar stripes; he was younger than Captain DeLongPre. He smiled and said, "This is your Captain speaking, friends—Captain Harkness. The ship will remain at one gravity for a little more than four hours.

I think it is time to serve lunch, don't you?"

He grinned again and I realized that my stomach wasn't bothering me at all—except that I was terribly hungry. I guess he knew that all of us ground hogs would be starving to death as soon as we were back to normal weight. He went on:

"We'll try to serve you just as quickly as possible. It is all right for you to unstrap now, sit up, and relax, but I must ask you to be very careful about one thing:

"This ship is precisely balanced so that the thrust of our drive passes exactly through our center of gravity. If that were not so, we would tend to spin instead of moving in a straight line—and we might fetch up in the heart of the Sun instead of at Ganymede.

"None of us wants to become an impromptu barbecue, so I will ask each of you not to move unnecessarily from the neighborhood of your couch. The ship has an automatic compensator for a limited amount of movement, but we must not overload it—so get permission from your ship's aide before moving as much as six inches from your present positions."

He grinned again and it was suddenly a most unpleasant grin. "Any one violating this rule will be strapped down by force—and the Captain will assign punishment to fit the crime after we are no longer under drive."

There wasn't any ship's aide in our compartment; all we could do was wait. I got acquainted with the boys in the bunkroom, some older, some younger. There was a big, sandy-haired boy about seventeen, by the name of Edwards—"Noisy" Edwards. He got tired of waiting.

I didn't blame him; it seemed like hours went past and still nothing to eat. I thought we had been forgotten.

Edwards had been hanging around the door, peering out. Finally he said, "This is ridiculous! We can't sit here all day. I'm for finding out what's the hold up. Who's with me?"

One of the fellows objected, "The Captain said to sit tight."

"What if he did? And what can he do if we don't? We aren't part of the crew."

I pointed out that the Captain had authority over the whole ship, but he brushed me off. "Tommyrot! We got a right to know what's going on—and a right to be fed. Who's coming along?"

Another boy said, "You're looking for trouble, Noisy."

Edwards stopped; I think he was worried by the remark but he couldn't back down. Finally he said, "Look, we're supposed to have a ship's aide and we haven't got one. You guys elect me ship's aide and I'll go bring back chow. How's that?"

Nobody objected out loud. Noisy said, "Okay, here I go."

He couldn't have been gone more than a few seconds when a ship's aide showed up carrying a big box of packaged rations. He dealt them out and had one left over. Then he counted the bunks. "Weren't there twenty boys in here?" he asked.

We looked at each other but nobody said anything. He pulled out a list and called our names. Edwards didn't answer, of course, and he left, taking Noisy's ration with him.

Then Noisy showed up and saw us eating and wanted to know where his lunch was. We told him; he said, "For the love of Mike! Why didn't you guys save it for me? A fine bunch you turned out to be." And he left again.

He came back shortly, looking mad. A ship's aide followed him and strapped him down.

We had about reached the teeth-picking stage when the screen on the ceiling lit up again and there was the Moon. It looked as if we were headed right toward it and coming up fast. I began to wonder if Captain Harkness had dropped a decimal point.

I lay back on my couch and watched it grow. After

a while it looked worse. When it had grown until it filled the screen and more and it seemed as if we couldn't possibly miss, I saw that the mountains were moving past on the screen from right to left. I breathed a sigh of relief; maybe the Old Man knew what he was doing after all.

A voice came over the speaker: "We are now passing the Moon and tacking slightly in so doing. Our relative speed at point of closest approach is more than fifty miles per second, producing a somewhat spectacular effect."

I'll say it was spectacular! We zipped across the face of the Moon in about half a minute, then it faded behind us. I suppose they simply kept a TV camera trained on it, but it looked as if we had dived in, turned sharply, and raced out again. Only you don't make sharp turns at *that* speed.

About two hours later they stopped gunning her. I had fallen asleep and I dreamed I was making a parachute jump and the chute failed to open. I woke up with a yell, weightless, with my stomach dropping out of me again. It took me a moment to figure out where I was.

The loudspeaker said: "End of acceleration. Spin will be placed on the ship at once."

But it did not happen all at once; it happened very slowly. We drifted toward one wall and slid down it toward the outer wall of the ship. That made what had been the outer wall the floor; we stood on it— and the side with the bunks on it was now a wall and the side with the TV screen on it, which had been the ceiling, was now the opposite wall. Gradually we got heavier.

Noisy was still strapped to his couch; the ship's aide had moved the buckles so that he could not reach them himself. Now he was up against the wall, hanging on the straps like a papoose. He began to yell for us to help him down.

He was not in any danger and he could not have

been too uncomfortable, for we weren't up to a full gravity, not by a whole lot. It turned out later that the Captain had brought the spin up to one-third g and held it there, because Ganymede has one-third g. So there wasn't any urgent need to turn Noisy loose.

Nor was there any rush to do so. We were still discussing it and some of the fellows were making comical remarks which Noisy did not appreciate when the same ship's aide came in, unstrapped Noisy, and told all of us to follow him.

That's how I happened to attend Captain's mast.

"Captain's mast" is a sort of court, like when in ancient times the lord of the countryside would sit and dispense the high and middle justice. We followed the aide, whose name was Dr. Archibald, to Captain Harkness's cabin. There were a lot of other people waiting there in the passage outside the cabin. Presently Captain Harkness came out and Noisy was the first case.

We were all witnesses but the Captain didn't question but a few of us; I wasn't questioned. Dr. Archibald told about finding Noisy wandering around the ship while we were under acceleration and the Captain asked Noisy if he had heard the order to stay at his bunk?

Noisy beat around the bush a good deal and tried to spread the blame on all of us, but when the Captain pinned him down he had to admit that he had heard the order.

Captain Harkness said, "Son, you are an undisciplined lunk. I don't know what sort of trouble you'll run into as a colonist, but so far as my ship is concerned, you've had it."

He mused for a moment, than added, "You say you did this because you were hungry?"

Noisy said yes, he hadn't had anything since breakfast and he still hadn't had his lunch.

"Ten days bread and water," said the Captain. "Next case."

Noisy looked as if he couldn't believe his ears.

The next case was the same thing, but a woman— one of those large, impressive ones who run things. She had had a row with her ship's aide and had stomped off to tell the Captain about it personally— while we were under acceleration.

Captain Harkness soon cut through the fog. "Madam," he said, with icy dignity, "by your bull-headed stupidity you have endangered the lives of all of us. Do you have anything to say for yourself?"

She started a tirade about how "rude" the aide had been to her and how she never heard of anything so preposterous in her life as this kangaroo court, and so forth, and so forth. The Captain cut her short.

"Have you ever washed dishes?" he asked.

"Why, no!"

"Well, you are going to wash dishes—for the next four hundred million miles."

6. $E = MC^2$

I looked up dad after they let us go. It was like finding a needle in a haystack but I kept asking and
presently I found him. Molly and he had a room to
themselves. Peggy was there and I thought she was
rooming with them, which annoyed me some, until I
saw that there were only two couches and realized
that Peggy must be in a dormitory. It turned out that
all the kids over eight were in dormitories.

Dad was busy unclamping their couches and moving
them to what was the floor, now that the ship was
spinning. He stopped when I came in and we sat
around and talked. I told him about Captain's mast.
He nodded. "We saw it in the screen. I didn't notice
your shining face, however."

I said I hadn't been called on.

"Why not?" Peggy wanted to know.

"How should I know?" I thought about mast for a
bit and said, "Say, George, the skipper of a ship in
space is just about the last of the absolute monarchs,
isn't he?"

Dad considered it and said, "Mmm . . . no, he's a
constitutional monarch. But he's a monarch all right."

"You mean we have to bow down to him and say
'Your Majesty'?" Peggy wanted to know.

Molly said, "I don't think that would be advisable, Peg."

"Why not? I think it would be fun."

Molly smiled. "Well, let me know how you make out. I suspect that he will just turn you over his knee and paddle you."

"Oh, he wouldn't dare! I'd scream."

I wasn't so sure. I remembered those four hundred million miles of dirty dishes. I decided that, if the Captain said "Frog," I'd hop.

If Captain Harkness was a monarch, he didn't seem anxious to rule; the first thing he had us do was to hold an election and set up a ship's council. After that we hardly laid eyes on him.

Everybody over eighteen could vote. The rest of us got to vote, too; we were told to set up a junior council—not that it was ever good for anything.

But the senior council, the *real* council, ran the ship from then on. It even acted as a court and the Captain never handed out punishments again. Dad told me that the Captain reviewed everything that the council did, that he *had* to, to make it legal—but I never heard of him overruling their decisions.

And you know what the first thing was that that council did—after setting up meal hours and simple things like that? They decided we had to go to school!

The junior council promptly held a meeting and passed a resolution against it, but it didn't mean anything. We had school, just the same.

Peggy was on the junior council. I asked her why she didn't resign if she wasn't going to do anything. I was just teasing—as a matter of fact she put up quite a battle for us.

School wasn't so bad, though. There is very little to do in space and when you've seen one star you've seen 'em all. And the first thing we had in school was a tour of the ship, which was all right.

We went in groups of twenty and it took all day—
"day" by ship's time, I mean. The *Mayflower* was
shaped like a ball with a cone on one side—top shaped.
The point of the cone was her jet—although Chief
Engineer Ortega, who showed us around, called it her
"torch."

If you count the torch end as her stern, then the
round end, her bow, was where the control room was
located; around it were the Captain's cabin and the
staterooms of the officers. The torch and the whole
power plant space were cut off from the rest of the
ship by a radiation shield that ran right through the
ship. From the shield forward to the control room
was a big cargo space. It was a cylinder more than a
hundred feet in diameter and was split up into holds.
We were carrying all sorts of things out to the colony
—earth moving machinery, concentrated soil cultures, instruments, I don't know what all.

Wrapped around this central cylinder were the
decks for living, "A" deck just inside the skin of the
ship, "B" deck under it, and "C" deck just inside that,
with "D" deck's ceiling being the outer wall of the
cargo space. "D" deck was the mess rooms and galley
and recreation rooms and sick bay and such; the
three outer decks were bunk rooms and staterooms.
"A" deck had steps in it every ten or fifteen feet because it was fitted into the outer curve of the ship;
this made the ceilings in it of various heights. The
furthest forward and furthest aft on "A" deck were
only about six feet between floor and ceiling and some
of the smaller kids lived in them, while at the greatest width of the ship the ceilings in "A" deck must
have been twelve or thirteen feet high.

From inside the ship it was hard to see how it all
fitted together. Not only was it all chopped up, but
the artificial gravity we had from spinning the ship
made directions confusing—anywhere you stood on a
deck it seemed level, but it curved sharply up behind
you and in front of you. But you never came to the

curved part; if you walked forward it was still level. If you walked far enough you looped the loop and came back to where you started, having walked clear around the ship.

I never would have figured it out if Mr. Ortega hadn't drawn a sketch for us.

Mr. Ortega told us that the ship was spinning three and six-tenths revolutions per minute or two hundred and sixteen complete turns an hour, which was enough to give "B" deck a centrifugal force of one-third g. "B" deck was seventy-five feet out from the axis of the *Mayflower*; "A" deck where I lived was further out and you weighed maybe a tenth more there, while "C" deck caught about a tenth less. "D" deck was quite a lot less and you could make yourself dizzy if you stood up suddenly in the mess room.

The control room was right on the axis; you could float in it even when the ship was spinning—or so they told me; I never was allowed inside.

Spinning the ship had another odd effect: all around us was "down." I mean to say that the only place you could put a view port was in the floor plates of "A" deck and that's where they were, four of them—big ones, each in its own compartment.

Mr. Ortega took us into one of these view galleries. The view port was a big round quartz plate in the floor, with a guard rail around it.

The first ones into the room went up to the guard rail and then backed away from it quick and two of the girls squealed. I pushed forward and got to the rail and looked down . . . and I was staring straight into the very bottom of the universe, a million trillion miles away and all of it *down*.

I didn't shy away—George says I'm more acrobat than acrophobe—but I did sort of grip the railing. Nobody wants to fall that far. The quartz was surface-treated so that it didn't give off reflections and it looked as if there were nothing at all between you and Kingdom Come.

The stars were reeling across the hole from the ship spinning, which made it worse. The Big Dipper came swinging in from the left, passed almost under me, and slid away to the right—and a few seconds later it was back again. I said, "This is where I came in," and gave up my place so that someone else could have a look, but nobody seemed anxious to.

Then we went through the hydroponics plant, but there wasn't anything fancy about that—just enough plants growing to replace the oxygen we used up breathing. Eel grass, it was mostly, but there was a vegetable garden as well. I wondered how they had gotten it going before they had the passengers aboard? Mr. Ortega pointed to a CO_2 fitting in the wall. "We had to subsidize them, of course."

I guess I should have known it; it was simple arithmetic.

The Chief led us back into one of the mess rooms, we sat down, and he told us about the power plant.

He said that there had been three stages in the development of space ships: first was the chemical fuel rocket ship that wasn't very different from the big German war rockets used in the Second World War, except that they were step rockets. "You kids are too young to have seen such rockets," he said, "but they were the biggest space ships ever built. They had to be big because they were terribly inefficient. As you all know, the first rocket to reach the Moon was a four-stage rocket. Its final stage was almost as long as the *Mayflower*—yet its pay load was less than a ton.

"It is characteristic of space ship development that the ships have gotten smaller instead of bigger. The next development was the atom-powered rocket. It was a great improvement; steps were no longer necessary. That meant that a ship like the *Daedalus* could take off from Earth without even a catapult, much less step rockets, and cruise to the Moon or even to Mars. But such ships still had the shortcomings of rockets; they depended on an atomic power plant to heat up reaction mass and push it out a jet, just as their predecessors depended on chemical fuel for the same purpose.

"The latest development is the mass-conversion ship, such as the *Mayflower*, and it may be the final development—a mass-conversion ship is theoretically capable of approaching the speed of light. Take this trip: we accelerated at one gravity for about four hours and twenty minutes which brought us up to more than ninety miles a second. If we had *held* that drive for a trifle less than a year, we would approach the speed of light.

"A mass-conversion ship has plenty of power to do just that. At one hundred per cent efficiency, it would use up about one per cent of her mass as energy and another one per cent as reaction mass. That's what the *Star Rover* is going to do when it is finished."

One of the younger kids was waving his hand. "Mister Chief Engineer?"

"Yes, son?"

"Suppose it goes on a few weeks longer and *passes* the speed of light?"

Mr. Ortega shook his head. "It can't."

"Why not, sir?"

"Eh, how far have you gone in mathematics, sonny?"

"Just through grammer school calculus," the kid answered.

"I'm afraid there is no use in trying to explain it, then. Just take it from me that the big brains are sure it can't be done."

I had worried about that very point more than once. Why *can't* you go faster than light? I know all that old double-talk about how the Einstein equations show that a speed faster than light is a meaningless quantity, like the weight of a song or the color of a sound, because it involves the square root of minus one—but all of that is just theory and if the course we had in history of science means anything at all, it means that scientists change their theories about as often as a snake changes his skin. I stuck up my hand.

"Okay," he says. "You with the cowlick. Speak up."

"Mr. Ortega, admitting that you can't pass the speed of light, what would happen if the *Star Rover* got up close to the speed of light—and then the Captain suddenly stepped the drive up to about six g and held it there?"

"Why, it would—— No, let's put it this way——" He broke off and grinned; it made him look real young. "See here, kid, don't ask me questions like that. I'm an engineer with hairy ears, not a mathematical physicist." He looked thoughtful and added, "Truthfully, I don't know what would happen, but I would sure give a pretty to find out. Maybe we would find out what the square root of minus one looks like—from the inside."

He went on briskly, "Let's go on about the *Mayflower*. You probably know that when the original *Star Rover* failed to come back, the *Mayflower* was designed to be the *Star Rover II,* but the design was obsolete before they ever started putting her together. So they shifted the name over to the new intersteller ship, the *Star Rover III,* renamed this one the *Mayflower* and grabbed her for the colonial service.

"You kids should consider how lucky you are. Up to now, emigrants to Ganymede have had to spend two years and nine months in space, just to get there. You're making it in two months."

"Couldn't we go faster?" somebody wanted to know.

"We could," he told us. "But we don't need to and it runs up the astrogation and control difficulties. In these new ships the power plant has gotten 'way ahead of the instrumentation. Be patient; your grandchildren will make the trip in a week, blasting at one g all the way. There'll be so many ships they'll have to have traffic cops and maybe we can come close to shipping out as many people as there are extras born each year.

"Enough about that," he went on. "Who here can tell me what 'E equals M C squared' means?"

I could have answered but I had already spoken up once and it doesn't do to get a reputation for apple polishing. Finally one of the older kids said, "It means that mass can be converted into energy."

"Right!" Mr. Ortega agreed. "The first real demonstration of that was the atom bomb they set off 'way back in 1945 at Alamogordo, New Mexico. That was a special case; they still didn't know how to control it; all they could do was to make one whale of a big bang. Then came the uranium power plants, but that still didn't amount to much because it was a very special case and only a microscopic percentage of the mass was converted into energy. It wasn't until Kilgore's energy transformation equations—don't worry about them; you'll study them when you are older if you are interested—it wasn't until Kilgore showed how it could be done that we had any idea of *how* to do what Dr. Einstein's energy-mass equation said, clear back in 1905.

"And we still didn't know how to control it. If we were going to turn mass into energy, we needed more mass with which to surround the reaction, a very special sort of mass that would not turn into energy when we didn't want it to and would hold the reaction where we wanted it. Ordinary metal wouldn't do; one might as well use soft butter.

"But the Kilgore equations showed how to do that, too, when they were read correctly. Now has anyone here any notion of how much energy you get when you convert a chunk of mass into raw energy?"

Nobody knew. "It's all in that one equation," he said, "good old Doc Einstein's 'E equals M C squared.' It comes out that one gram of mass gives nine times ten to the twentieth power ergs." He wrote it down for us: 1 gm. = 9×10^{20} ergs.

"Doesn't look like much, does it?" he said. "Now try it this way:" He wrote down

900,000,000,000,000,000,000 ergs.

"Read it off. Nine hundred thousand million billion ergs. It still doesn't mean much, does it? Figures like that are impossible to comprehend. The nuclear physicists keep a barrel of zeroes around handy the way a carpenter does a keg of nails.

"I'll try once more," he went on. "A pound of mass, any old mass, say a pound of feathers, when converted into energy equals *fifteen billion* horsepower-hours. Does that give anyone a notion of why the *Mayflower* was assembled out in an orbit and will never ever land anywhere?"

"Too hot," somebody said.

"'Too hot' is an understatement. If the *Mayflower* had blasted off from Mojave space port the whole Los Angeles Borough of the City of Southern California would have been reduced to a puddle of lava and people would have been killed by radiation and heat from Bay City to Baja California. And that will give you an idea of why the shielding runs right through the ship between here and the power plant, with no way at all to get at the torch."

We had the misfortune to have Noisy Edwards along, simply because he was from the same bunk room. Now he spoke up and said, "Suppose you have to make a repair?"

"There is nothing to go wrong," explained Mr. Ortega. "The power plant has no moving parts of any sort."

Noisy wasn't satisfied. "But suppose something did go wrong, how would you fix it if you can't get at it?"

Noisy has an irritating manner at best; Mr. Ortega sounded a little impatient when he answered. "Believe me, son, even if you could get at it, you wouldn't want to. No indeed!"

"Humph!" said Noisy. "All I've got to say is, if there isn't any way to make a repair when a repair is needed, what's the use in sending engineer officers along?"

You could have heard a pin drop. Mr. Ortega turned red, but all he said was, "Why, to answer foolish questions from youngsters like yourself, I suppose." He turned to the rest of us. "Any more questions?"

Naturally nobody wanted to ask any then. He added, "I think that's enough for one session. School's out."

I told Dad about it later. He looked grim and said, "I'm afraid Chief Engineer Ortega didn't tell you the whole truth."

"Huh?"

"In the first place there is plenty for him to do in taking care of the auxiliary machinery on this side of the shield. But it is possible to get at the torch, if necessary."

"Huh? How?"

"There are certain adjustments which could conceivably have to be made in extreme emergency. In which case it would be Mr. Ortega's proud privilege to climb into a space suit, go outside and back aft, and make them."

"You mean——"

"I mean that the assistant chief engineer would succeed to the position of chief a few mintues later. Chief engineers are very carefully chosen, Bill, and not just for their technical knowledge."

It made me feel chilly inside; I didn't like to think about it.

7. Scouting in Space

Making a trip in a space ship is about the dullest way to spend time in the world, once the excitement wears off. There's no scenery, nothing to do, and no room to do it in. There were nearly six thousand of us crowded into the *Mayflower* and that doesn't leave room to swing a cat.

Take "B" deck—there were two thousand passengers sleeping in it. It was 150 feet across—fore and aft, that is—and not quite 500 feet around, cylinder fashion. That gives about forty square feet per passenger, on the average, but a lot was soaked up in stairs, passageways, walls, and such. It worked out that each one had about room enough for his bunk and about that much left over to stand on when he wasn't sleeping.

You can't give a rodeo in that kind of space; you can't even get up a game of ring-around-the-rosy.

"A" deck was larger and "C" deck was smaller, being nearer the axis, but they averaged out the same. The council set up a staggered system to get the best use out of the galley and the mess rooms and to keep us from falling over each other in the 'freshers. "A" deck was on Greenwich time; "B" deck was left on zone plus-eight time, or Pacific West Coast time; and "C" deck drew zone minus-eight time, Philippine time.

That would have put us on different days, of course, but the day was always figured officially on Greenwich time; the dodge was just to ease the pressure on eating facilities.

That was really all we had to worry about. You would wake up early, not tired but bored, and wait for breakfast. Once breakfast was over, the idea was to kill time until lunch. All afternoon you could look forward to the terrific excitement of having dinner.

I have to admit that making us go to school was a good plan; it meant that two and a half hours every morning and every afternoon was taken care of. Some of the grown ups complained that the mess rooms and all the spare space was always crowded with classes, but what did they expect us to do? Go hang on sky hooks? We used up less space in class than if we had been under foot.

Still, it was a mighty odd sort of school. There were some study machines in the cargo but we couldn't get at them and there wouldn't have been enough to go around. Each class consisted of about two dozen kids and some adult who knew something about something. (You'd be surprised how many adults don't know anything about anything!) The grown up would talk about what he knew best and the kids would listen, then we would ask questions and he would ask questions. No real examinations, no experiments, no demonstrations, no stereos.

Dad says this is the best kind of a school, that a university consists of a log with a teacher on one end and a pupil on the other. But Dad is a sort of romantic.

Things got so dull that it was hardly worth while to keep up my diary, even if I had been able to get microfilm, which I wasn't.

Dad and I played an occasional game of cribbage in the evening—somehow Dad had managed to squeeze the board and a pack of cards into his weight allowance. Then he got too busy with technical planning he was doing for the council and didn't have time. Molly suggested that I teach her to play, so I did.

After that I taught Peggy to play and she pegged a pretty sharp game, for a girl. It worried me a little that I wasn't being loyal to Anne in getting chummy with Peg and her mother, but I decided that Anne would want me to do just what I did. Anne was always friendly with everybody.

It still left me with time on my hands. What with only one-third gravity and no exercise I couldn't sleep more than six hours a night. The lights were out eight hours but they didn't make us go to bed, not after the trouble they had with it the first week. I used to fool around the corridors after lights out, usually with Hank Jones, until we both would get sleepy. We talked a lot. Hank turned out not to be such a bad guy as long as you kept him trimmed down to size.

I still had my Scout suit with me and kept it folded up in my bunk. Hank came in one morning while I was making up my bunk and noticed it. "See here, William," he said, "why do you hang on to that? Let the dead past bury its dead."

"I don't know," I admitted. "Maybe there will be Scouting on Ganymede."

"Not that I ever heard of."

"Why not? There is Scouting on the Moon."

"Proves nothing," he answered.

But it got us to talking about it and Hank got a brilliant idea. Why not start up Scouting right now, in the *Mayflower*?

We called a meeting. Peggy spread the word around for us, through the junior council, and we set it for fifteen-thirty that same afternoon, right after school. Fifteen-thirty Greenwich, or "A" deck time, that is. That made it seven-thirty in the morning for the "B" deck boys and a half hour before mid-night for the fellows on "C" deck. It was the best we could do. "B" deck could hurry through breakfast and get to the meeting if they wanted to and we figured that those who were really interested from "C" would stay up for the meeting.

I played my accordion while they were drifting in because Hank's father said that you needed music to warm up a meeting before it got down to work. The call had read "all Scouts and former Scouts;" by fifteen-forty we had them packed in and spilling into the corridors, even though we had the use of the biggest mess room. Hank called them to order and I put away my accordion and acted as Scribe *pro tem*, having borrowed a wire recorder from the Communications Officer for the purpose.

Hank made a little speech. I figure him for politics when he grows up. He said that all of us had enjoyed the benefits, the comradeship, and the honorable traditions of Scouting on Earth and it seemed a shame to lose them. He said that the Scouting tradition was the tradition of the explorer and pioneer and there could be no more fitting place and time for it than in the settlement of a new planet. In fact the spirit of Daniel Boone demanded that we continue as Scouts.

I didn't know he had it in him. It sounded good.

He stopped and slipped me the wink. I got up and said that I wanted to propose a resolution. Then I read it—it had been a lot longer but we cut it down. It read: "Be it resolved—we the undersigned, Scouts and former Scouts of many jurisdictions and now passengers in the good ship *Mayflower*, having as our purpose to continue the Scouting tradition and to extend the Scouting trail out to the stars, do organize ourselves as the Boy Scouts of Ganymede in accordance with the principles and purpose of Scouting and in so doing do reaffirm the Scout Law."

Maybe it was flowery but it sounded impressive; nobody laughed. Hank said, "You have heard the resolution; what is your pleasure? Do I hear a second?"

He surely did; there were seconds all over the place. Then he asked for debate.

Somebody objected that we couldn't call ourselves

the Boy Scouts of Ganymede because we weren't on Ganymede yet. He got a chilly reception and shut up. Then somebody else pointed out that Ganymede wasn't a star, which made that part about "Carrying the Scouting trail out to the stars" nonsense.

Hank told him that was poetic license and anyhow going out to Ganymede was a step in the right direction and that there would be more steps; what about the *Star Rover III?* That shut *him* up.

The worst objection was from "Millimetre" Muntz, a weary little squirt too big for his britches. He said, "Mr. Chairman, this is an outlaw meeting. You haven't any authority to set up a new Scouting jurisdiction. As a member in good standing of Troop Ninety-Six, New Jersey, I object to the whole proceeding."

Hank asked him just what authority he thought Troop Ninety-Six, New Jersey, had out around the orbit of Mars? Somebody yelled, "Throw him out!"

Hank banged on the mess table. "It isn't necessary to throw him out—but, since Brother Millimetre thinks this is not a proper meeting, then it isn't proper for him to take part in it. He is excused and the chair will recognize him no further. Are you ready to vote?"

It was passed unanimously and then Hank was elected organizational chairman. He appointed a flock of committees, for organization and for plans and programs and for credentials and tests and for liaison, and such. That last was to dig out the men in the ship who had been troop masters and commissioners and things and get a Court of Honor set up. There were maybe a dozen of the men passengers at the meeting, listening. One of them, a Dr. Archibald who was an aide on "A" deck, spoke up.

"Mr. Chairman, I was a Scoutmaster in Nebraska. I'd like to volunteer my services to this new organization."

Hank looked him straight in the eye. "Thank you, sir. Your application will be considered."

Dr. Archibald looked startled, but Hank went

smoothly on, "We want and need and will appreciate the help of all you older Scouts. The liaison committee is instructed to get the names of any who are willing to serve."

It was decided that we would have to have three troops, one for each deck, since it wasn't convenient to try to meet all at the same time. Hank asked all the Explorer Scouts to stand up. There were too many of them, so he asked those who were Eagles to remain standing. There were about a dozen of us.

Hank separated us Eagles by decks and told us to get busy and organize our troops and to start by picking an acting senior patrol leader. "A" deck had only three Eagles, me, Hank, and a kid from another bunk room whom I hadn't met before, Douglas MacArthur Okajima. Doug and Hank combined on me and I found myself tagged with the job.

Hank and I had planned to finish the meeting with setting up exercises, but there just wasn't room, so I got out my accordion again and we sang *The Scouting Trail* and followed it with *The Green Hills of Earth*. Then we took the oath together again:

"Upon my honor I will do my best to do my duty to God and my planet, and to keep myself physically fit, mentally alert, and morally straight."

After that the meeting busted up.

For a while we held meetings every day. Between troop meetings and committee meetings and Explorer meetings and patrol leader meetings we didn't have time to get bored. At first the troops were just "A" troop, "B" troop, and "C" troop, after the decks, but we wanted names to give them some personality. Anyhow I wanted a name for my troop; we were about to start a membership drive and I wanted something with more oomph to it than " 'A' deck troop."

Somebody suggested "The Space Rats" but that was voted down, and somebody else suggested "The Mayflowers"; they didn't bother to vote on that; they simply sat on him.

After that we turned down "The Pilgrims," "Deep Space Troop," "Star Rovers," and "Sky High." A kid named John Edward Forbes-Smith got up. "Look," he said, "we're divided into three troops on the basis of the time zones we use, aren't we? "B" deck has California time; "C" deck has Philippine time; and we have Greenwich or English time. Why don't we pick names that will show that fact? We could call ourselves the Saint George Troop."

Bud Kelly said it was a good idea as far as it went but make it Saint Patrick instead of Saint George; after all, Dublin was on Greenwich time, too, and Saint Patrick was a more important saint.

Forbes-Smith said, "Since when?"

Bud said, "Since always, you limey—" So we sat on both of them, too, and it was decided not to use saints. But Johnny Edwards had a good idea, just the same; we settled on the Baden-Powell Troop, Boy Scouts of Ganymede, which tied in with the English time zone and didn't offend anybody.

The idea took hold; "C" deck picked Aguinaldo as a name and "B" deck called themselves the Junipero Serra Troop. When I heard that last I was kind of sorry our deck didn't have California time so that we could have used it. But I got over it; after all "Baden-Powell" is a mighty proud name, too.

For that matter they were all good names—scouts and explorers and brave men, all three of them. Two of them never had a chance to be Scouts in the narrow, organized meaning, but they were all Scouts in the wider sense—like Daniel Boone.

Dad says there is a lot in a name.

As soon as they heard about what we were doing the girls set up Girl Scouting, too, and Peggy was a member of the Florence Nightingale Troop. I suppose there was no harm in it, but why do girls copy what the boys do? We were too busy to worry about them, though; we had to revamp Scouting activities to fit new conditions.

We decided to confirm whatever ranks and badges a boy had held in his former organization—permanent rankings, I mean, not offices. Having been a patrol leader or a scribe didn't mean anything, but if you were an Eagle on Earth, you stayed one in the B.S.G.; if you were a Cub, then you were still a Cub. If a boy didn't have records—and about half of them didn't— we took his Scout oath statement as official.

That was simple; working over the tests and the badges was complicated. After all you can't expect a boy to pass bee-keeping when you haven't any bees.

(It turned out that there *were* several swarms of bees sleep-frozen in the cargo, but we didn't have the use of them.)

But we could set up a merit badge in hydroponics and give tests right there in the ship. And Mr. Ortega set up a test for us in spaceship engineering and Captain Harkness did the same for ballistics and astrogation. By the end of the trip we had enough new tests to let a boy go up for Eagle Scout, once we had a Court of Honor.

That came last. For some reason I couldn't figure Hank had kept putting off the final report of the liaison committee, the committee which had as its job getting Scout Masters and Commissioners and such. I asked him about it, but he just looked mysterious and said that I would see.

I did see, eventually. At last we had a joint meeting of all three troops to install Scout Masters and dedicate the Court of Honor and such. And from then on the adults ran things and we went back to being patrol leaders at the most. Oh well—it was fun while it lasted.

8.   Trouble

When we were fifty-three days out and about a week to go to reach Ganymede, Captain Harkness used the flywheel to precess the ship so that we could see where we were going—so that the passengers could see, that is; it didn't make any difference to his astrogation.

You see, the axis of the *Mayflower* had been pointed pretty much toward Jupiter and the torch had been pointed back at the Sun. Since the view ports were spaced every ninety degrees around the sides, while we had been able to see most of the sky, we hadn't been able to see ahead to Jupiter nor behind to the Sun. Now he tilted the ship over ninety degrees and we were rolling, so to speak, along our line of flight. That way, you could see Jupiter and the Sun both, from any view port, though not both at the same time.

Jupiter was already a tiny, ruddy-orange disc. Some of the boys claimed they could make out the moons. Frankly, I couldn't, not for the first three days after the Captain precessed the ship. But it was mighty fine to be able to see Jupiter.

We hadn't seen Mars on the way out, because Mars happened to be on the far side of the Sun, three hundred million miles away. We hadn't seen anything but the same old stars you can see from Earth. We didn't even see any asteroids.

There was a reason for that. When we took off from the orbit of Supra-New-York, Captain Harkness had not aimed the *Mayflower* straight for where Jupiter was going to be when we got there; instead he had lifted her north of the ecliptic high enough to give the asteroid belt a wide berth. Now anybody knows that meteors are no real hazard in space. Unless a pilot does deliberately foolish things like driving his ship through the head of a comet it is almost impossible to get yourself hit by a meteor. They are too far between.

On the other hand the asteroid belt has more than its fair share of sky junk. The older power-pile ships used to drive straight through the belt, taking their chances, and none of them was ever hit to amount to anything. But Captain Harkness, having literally all the power in the world, preferred to go around and play it safe. By avoiding the belt there wasn't a chance in a blue moon that the *Mayflower* would be hit.

Well, it must have been a blue moon. We were hit.

It was just after reveille, "A" deck time, and I was standing by my bunk, making it up. I had my Scout uniform in my hands and was about to fold it up and put it under my pillow. I still didn't wear it. None of the others had uniforms to wear to Scout meetings so I didn't wear mine. But I still kept it tucked away in my bunk.

Suddenly I heard the goldarnest noise I ever heard in my life. It sounded like a rifle going off right by my ear, it sounded like a steel door being slammed, and it sounded like a giant tearing yards and yards of cloth, all at once.

Then I couldn't hear anything but a ringing in my ears and I was dazed. I shook my head and looked down and I was staring at a raw hole in the ship, almost between my feet and nearly as big as my fist.

There was scorched insulation around it and in the middle of the hole I could see blackness—then a star whipped past and I realized that I was staring right out into space.

There was a hissing noise.

I don't remember thinking at all. I just wadded up my uniform, squatted down, and stuffed it in the hole. For a moment it seemed as if the suction would pull it on through the hole, then it jammed and stuck and didn't go any further. But we were still losing air. I think that was the point at which I first realized that we *were* losing air and that we might be suffocated in vacuum.

There was somebody yelling and screaming behind me that he was killed and alarm bells were going off all over the place. You couldn't hear yourself think. The air-tight door to our bunk room slid across automatically and settled into its gaskets and we were locked in.

That scared me to death.

I know it has to be done. I know that it is better to seal off one compartment and kill the people who are in it than to let a whole ship die—but, you see, *I* was in that compartment, personally. I guess I'm just not the hero type.

I could feel the pressure sucking away at the plug my uniform made. With one part of my mind I was recalling that it had been advertised as "tropical weave, self ventilating" and wishing that it had been a solid plastic rain coat instead. I was afraid to stuff it in any harder, for fear it would go all the way through and leave us sitting there, chewing vacuum. I would have passed up desserts for the next ten years for just one rubber patch, the size of my hand.

The screaming had stopped; now it started up again. It was Noisy Edwards, beating on the air-tight door and yelling, "Let me out of here! *Get me out of here!*"

On top of that I could hear Captain Harkness's voice coming through the bull horn. He was saying,

"H-twelve! Report! H-twelve! Can you hear me?"

On top of that everybody was talking at once.

I yelled: "Quiet!" at the top of my voice—and for a second or so there *was* quiet.

Peewee Brunn, one of my Cubs, was standing in front of me, looking big-eyed. "What happened, Billy?" he said.

I said, "Grab me a pillow off one of the bunks. Jump!"

He gulped and did it. I said, "Peel off the cover, quick!"

He did, making quite a mess of it, and handed it to me—but I didn't have a hand free. I said, "Put it down on top of my hands."

It was the ordinary sort of pillow, soft foam rubber. I snatched one hand out and then the other, and then I was kneeling on it and pressing down with the heels of my hands. It dimpled a little in the middle and I was scared we were going to have a blowout right through the pillow. But it held. Noisy was screaming again and Captain Harkness was still asking for somebody, *anybody*, in compartment H-12 to tell him what was going on. I yelled "*Quiet!*" again, and added, "Somebody slug Noisy and shut him up."

That was a popular idea. About three of them jumped to it. Noisy got clipped in the side of the neck, then somebody poked him in the pit of his stomach and they swarmed over him. "Now everybody keep quiet," I said, "and keep on keeping quiet. If Noisy lets out a peep, slug him again." I gasped and tried to take a deep breath and said, "H-twelve, reporting!"

The Captain's voice answered, "What is the situation there?"

"There is a hole in the ship, Captain, but we got it corked up."

"How? And how big a hole?"

I told him and that is about all there was to it. They took a while to get to us because—I found this out afterward—they isolated that stretch of corridor first, with the air-tight doors, and that meant they had to get everybody out of the rooms on each side of us and across the passageway. But presently two men in space suits opened the door and chased all the kids out, all but me. Then they came back. One of them was Mr. Ortega. "You can get up now, kid," he said, his voice sounding strange and far away through his helmet. The other man squatted down and took over holding the pillow in place.

Mr. Ortega had a big metal patch under one arm. It had sticky padding on one side. I wanted to stay and watch him put it on but he chased me out and closed the door. The corridor outside was empty but I banged on the air-tight door and they let me through to where the rest were waiting. They wanted to know what was happening but I didn't have any news for them because I had been chased out.

After a while we started feeling light and Captain Harkness announced that spin would be off the ship for a short time. Mr. Ortega and the other man came back and went on up to the control room. Spin was off entirely soon after that and I got very sick. Captain Harkness kept the ship's speaker circuits cut in on his conversations with the men who had gone outside to repair the hole, but I didn't listen. I defy anybody to be interested in anything when he is drop sick.

Then spin came back on and everything was all right and we were allowed to go back into our bunkroom. It looked just the same except that there was a plate welded over the place where the meteorite had come in.

Breakfast was two hours late and we didn't have school that morning.

That was how I happened to go up to Captain's mast for the second time. George was there and Molly and Peggy and Dr. Archibald, the Scoutmaster of our deck, and all the fellows from my bunk room and all the ship's officers. The rest of the ship was cut in by visiplate. I wanted to wear my uniform but it was a mess—torn and covered with sticky stuff. I finally cut off the merit badges and put it in the ship's incinerator.

The First Officer shouted, "Captain's Mast for punishments and rewards!" Everybody sort of straightened up and Captain Harkness walked out and faced us. Dad shoved me forward.

The Captain looked at me. "William Lermer?" he said.

I said, "Yessir.".

He said, "I will read from yesterday's log: 'On twenty-one August at oh-seven-oh-four system standard, while cruising in free fall according to plan, the ship was broached by a small meteorite. Safety interlocks worked satisfactorily and the punctured volume, compartment H-twelve, was isolated with no serious drop in pressure elsewhere in the ship.

" 'Compartment H-twelve is a bunk room and was occupied at the time of the emergency by twenty passengers. One of the passengers, William J. Lermer, contrived a makeshift patch with materials at hand and succeeded in holding sufficient pressure for breathing until a repair party could take over.

" 'His quick thinking and immediate action unquestionably saved the lives of all persons in compartment H-twelve.' "

The Captain looked up from the log and went on, "A certified copy of this entry, along with depositions of witnesses, will be sent to Interplanetary Red Cross with recommendation for appropriate action. Another copy will be furnished you. I have no way to reward you except to say that you have my heart-felt gratitude. I know that I speak not only for the officers but for all the passengers and most especially for the parents of your bunk mates."

He paused and waggled a finger for me to come closer. He went on in a low voice, to me alone, "That really was a slick piece of work. You were on your toes. You have a right to feel proud."

I said I guessed I had been lucky.

He said, "Maybe. But that sort of luck comes to the man who is prepared for it."

He waited a moment, then said, "Lermer, have you ever thought of putting in for space training?"

I said I suppose I had but I hadn't thought about it very seriously. He said, "Well, Lermer, if you ever do decide to, let me know. You can reach me care of the Pilots' Association, Luna City."

With that, mast was over and we went away, George and I together and Molly and Peggy following along. I heard Peggy saying, "That's *my* brother."

Molly said, "Hush, Peggy. And don't point."

Peggy said, "Why not? He *is* my brother—well, isn't he?"

Molly said, "Yes, but there's no need to embarrass him."

But I wasn't embarrassed.

Mr. Ortega looked me up later and handed me a little, black, twisted piece of metal, about as big as a button. "That's all there was left of it," he said, "but I thought you would like to have it—pay you for messing up your Scout suit, so to speak."

I thanked him and said I didn't mind losing the uniform; after all, it had saved my neck, too. I looked at the meteorite. "Mr. Ortega, is there any way to tell where this came from?"

"Not really," he told me, "though you can get the scientific johnnies to cut it up and then express an opinion—if you don't mind them destroying it."

I said no, I'd rather keep it—and I have; I've still got it as a pocket piece. He went on, "It's either a bit of a comet or a piece of the Ruined Planet. We can't tell which because where we were there shouldn't have been either one."

"Only there was," I said.

"As you say, there was."

"Uh, Mr. Ortega, why don't they put enough armor on a ship to stop a little bitty thing like this?" I remembered what the skin of the ship looked like where it had been busted; it seemed awful thin.

"Well, now, in the first place, this meteor is a real giant, as meteors go. In the second place—do you know anything about cosmic rays, Bill?"

"Uh, not much, I guess."

"You undoubtedly know that the human body is transparent to primary cosmic radiation and isn't harmed by it. That is what we encounter out here in space. But metal is not completely transparent to it and when it passes through metal it kicks up all sorts of fuss—secondary and tertiary and quaternary cosmic radiation. The stuff cascades and it is *not* harmless, not by a darn sight. It can cause mutations and do you and your descendants a lot of harm. It adds up to this: a man is safest in space when he has just enough ship around him to keep the air in and ultraviolet out."

Noisy didn't have much to say around the compartment for the next couple of days and I thought maybe he had learned his lesson. I was wrong. I ran into him in one of the lower passageways when there was nobody else around. I started to go around him but he stepped in my way. "I want to talk to you," he said.

"Okay," I answered. "What's on your mind?"

"You think you're pretty smart, don't you?"

I didn't like the way he said it, nor what he said. I said, "I don't *think* I'm smart; I *am* smart." He made me tired.

"Pretty cocky, aren't you? You think I ought to be kissing your hand and telling you how grateful I am for saving my life, don't you?"

I said, "Oh, yeah? If that's what is worrying you, you can just skip it; I didn't do it for *you.*"

"I know that," he answered," and I'm *not* grateful, see?"

"That's fine with me," I told him. "I wouldn't want a guy like you being grateful to me."

He was breathing hard. "I've had just about enough of you," he said slowly. And the next thing I knew I had a mouthful of knuckles and I was down.

I got up cautiously, trying to surprise him. But it was no good; he knocked me down again. I tried to kick him while I was down, but he danced out of my way.

The third time he hit me I stayed down. When I quit seeing stars he was gone—and I hadn't managed to lay a finger on him. I never was any good in a fight; I'm still talking when I ought to be slugging.

I went to a scuttlebutt and bathed my face. Hank ran across me there and asked me what in the world I had been doing. I told him I had run into a door. I told Dad the same thing.

Noisy didn't bother me any more and we never had anything to say to each other again. I lay awake a long time that night, trying to figure it out. I didn't get it. The chap who thought up that malarkey about "my strength is as the strength of ten because my heart is pure" certainly had never met Noisy Edwards. For my taste Noisy was a no good so-and-so and I wished I had been able to use his face to stuff the hole the meteor made. I thought about a number of ways to fix him, but none of them was any good. As Dad says, sometimes there just isn't any cure for a situation.

9. The Moons of Jupiter

Nothing much happened until it was time to make our approach to Jupiter, except that a four-year-old kid turned up missing. The kid's parents searched all around and they passed the word from the control room for everybody to keep an eye open but they still couldn't find him.

So we had a chance to try out the Scouts' emergency organization. The ship's officers couldn't search the ship, since there was just the Captain and two watch officers and Mr. Ortega and his assistant chief. Captain Harkness supplied plans to each of the Scoutmasters and we went through that ship like a kid searching his clothes for a half credit. We turned the kid up, all right, in about twenty minutes. Seems the little devil had snuck into the hydroponics room while it was being serviced and had got himself locked in.

While he was in there he had got thirsty and had tried to drink the solutions they raise the plants in—had drunk some, in fact. The result was just about what you would expect. It didn't do him any real harm but, boy, was that place a mess!

I was talking to Dad about it that night over a game. Peggy had a Girl Scout meeting and Molly was off somewhere; we were alone for once. The baby's mother had raised particular Ned, just as if there had really been something wrong—I mean, what can happen in a space ship? The kid couldn't fall overboard.

Dad said her reaction was perfectly natural.

I said, "See, here, George, does it seem to you that some of the emigrants don't have what it takes to be colonists?"

"Mmmm . . . possibly."

I was thinking of Noisy but the ones I mentioned were Mrs. Tarbutton, who gave up and didn't even come along, and that female—Mrs. Grigsby—who got in trouble and had to wash dishes. And another fellow named Saunders who was continually in trouble with the council for trying to live his own life, wild and free, no matter what it did to the rest of us. "George, how did those characters get past the psycho tests?"

George stopped to peg fifteen-four, then said, "Bill, haven't you ever heard of political influence?"

All I said was, "Huh?"

"It's a shocking thought I know, but you are old enough to get used to the world as it is, instead of the way it ought to be. Take a hypothetical case: I don't suppose that a niece of a state councilor would be very likely to fail the psycho tests. Oh, she might fail the first tests, but a review board might find differently— if the councilor really wanted her to pass."

I chewed this over a while. It did not sound like George; he isn't the cynical type. Me, I'm cynical, but George is usually naïve. "In that case, George, there is no use in having psycho tests at all, not if people like that can sneak past."

"Contrariwise. The tests are usually honest. As for those who sneak past, it doesn't matter. Old Mother Nature will take care of them in the long run. Survivors survive." He finished dealing and said, "Wait till you see what I'm going to do to you this hand. You haven't a chance."

He always says that. I said, "Anybody who would use public office like that ought to be impeached!"

George said mildly, "Yep. But don't burn out your jets, son; we've got human beings, not angels, to work with."

On the twenty-fourth of August Captain Harkness took spin off and started bringing us in. We decelerated for better than four hours and then went into free fall about six hundred thousand miles out from Jupiter and on the opposite side from where Ganymede was then. Weightlessness still wasn't any fun but this time we were ready and everyone got shots for it who wanted them. I took mine and no nonsense.

Theoretically the *Mayflower* could have made it in one compound maneuver, ending up at the end of deceleration in a tight circular orbit around Ganymede. Practically it was much better to sneak in easy and avoid any more trouble with meteorites—with the "false rings," that is.

Of course Jupiter doesn't have rings like Saturn, but it does have quite a lot of sky junk traveling around in the same plane as its moons. If there were enough of it, it would show up like Saturn's rings. There isn't that much, but there is enough to make a pilot walk on eggs coming in. This slow approach gave us a fine front seat for a tour of Jupiter and its satellites.

Most of this stuff we were trying to avoid is in the same plane as Jupiter's equator, just the way Saturn's rings are—so Captain Harkness brought us in *over the top* of Jupiter, right across Jupiter's north pole. That way, we never did get in the danger zone until we had curved down on the other side to reach Ganymede—and by then we were going fairly slow.

But we weren't going slow when we passed over Jupiter's north pole, no indeedy! We were making better than thirty miles a second and we were close in, about thirty thousand miles. It was quite a sight.

Jupiter is ninety thousand miles thick; thirty thousand miles is close—too close for comfort.

I got one good look at it for about two minutes from one of the view ports, then had to give up my place to somebody who hadn't had a turn yet and go back to the bunk room and watch through the vision screen. It was an odd sight; you always think of Jupiter with equatorial bands running parallel across it. But now we were looking at it end on and the bands were circles. It looked like a giant archery target, painted in orange and brick red and brown—except that half of it was chewed away. We saw it in half moon, of course.

There was a dark spot right at the pole. They said that was a zone of permanent clear weather and calm and that you could see clear down to the surface there. I looked but I couldn't see anything; it just looked dark.

As we came over the top, Io—that's satellite number one—suddenly came out of eclipse. Io is about as big as the Moon and was about as far away from us at the time as the Moon is from the Earth, so it looked about Moon size. There was just black sky and then there was a dark, blood red disc and in less than five minutes it was brilliant orange, about the color of Jupiter itself. It simply popped up, like magic.

I looked for Barnard's satellite while we were close in, but missed it. It's the little one that is less than one diameter from the surface of Jupiter—so close that it whirls around Jupiter in twelve hours. I was interested in it because I knew that the Jovian observatory was on it and also the base for Project Jove.

I probably didn't miss anything; Barnard's satellite is only about a hundred and fifty miles in diameter. They say a man can come pretty close to jumping right off it. I asked George about it and he said, no, the escape speed was about five hundred feet per second and who had been filling me up with nonsense?

I looked it up later; he was right. Dad is an absolute

mine of useless information. He says a fact should be loved for itself alone.

Callisto was behind us; we had passed her on the way in, but not very close. Europa was off to the right of our course nearly ninety degrees; we saw her in half moon. She was more than four hundred thousand miles away and was not as pretty a sight as the Moon is from Earth.

Ganymede was straight ahead, almost, and growing all the time—and here was a funny thing; Callisto was silvery, like the Moon, but not as bright; Io and Europa were bright orange, as bright as Jupiter itself. Ganymede was downright dull!

I asked George about it; he came through, as usual. "Ganymede used to be about as bright as Io and Europa," he told me. "It's the greenhouse effect—the heat trap. Otherwise we wouldn't be able to live on it."

I knew about that, of course; the greenhouse effect is the most important part of the atmosphere project. When the 1985 expedition landed Ganymede had a surface temperature a couple of hundred degrees below zero—that's cold enough to freeze the milk of human kindness! "But look, George," I objected, "sure, I know about the heat trap, but why is it so dark? It looks like the inside of a sack."

"Light is heat; heat is light," he answered. "What's the difference? It's not dark on the ground; it goes in and doesn't come out—and a good thing, too."

I shut up. It was something new to me and I didn't understand it, so I decided to wait and not pound my teeth about it.

Captain Harkness slowed her down again as we came up to Ganymede and we got in one good meal while she was under drive. I never did get so I could eat at free fall, even with injections. He leveled her off in a tight circular orbit about a thousand miles up from Ganymede. We had arrived—just as soon as we could get somebody to come and get us.

It was on the trip down to Ganymede's surface that I began to suspect that being a colonist wasn't as glamorous and romantic as it had seemed back on Earth. Instead of three ships to carry us all at once, there was just one ship, the *Jitterbug*, and she would have fitted into one of the *Bifrost's* compartments. She could carry only ninety of us at a time and that meant a lot of trips.

I was lucky; I had to wait only three days in free fall. But I lost ten pounds.

While I waited, I worked, helping to stow the freight that the *Jitterbug* brought up each trip. At last it came our turn and we piled into the *Jitterbug*. She was terrible; she had shelves rather than decks—they weren't four feet apart. The air was stale and she hadn't been half way cleaned up since the last trip. There weren't individual acceleration couches; there were just pads covering the deck space and *we* covered the pads, shoulder to shoulder—and foot in your eye, for that matter.

The skipper was a loud-mouthed old female they called "Captain Hattie" and she kept bawling us out and telling us to hurry. She didn't even wait to make sure that we were all strapped down.

Fortunately it didn't take very long. She drove away so hard that for the first time except in tests I blacked out, then we dropped for about twenty minutes; she gunned her again, and we landed with a terrible bump. And Captain Hattie was shouting, "Out you come, you ground hogs! This is it."

The *Jitterbug* carried oxygen, rather than the helium-oxygen mix of the *Mayflower*. We had come down at ten pounds pressure; now Captain Hattie spilled the pressure and let it adjust to Ganymede normal, three pounds. Sure, three pounds of oxygen is enough to live on; that's all Earth has—the other twelve pounds are nitrogen. But a sudden drop in pressure like that is enough to make you gasp anyhow. You aren't suffocating but you feel as if you were.

We were miserable by the time we got out and Peggy had a nose bleed. There weren't any elevators; we had to climb down a rope ladder. And it was cold!

It was snowing; the wind was howling around us and shaking the ladder—the smallest kids they had to lower with a line. There was about eight inches of snow on the ground except where the splash of the *Jitterbug's* jet had melted it. I could hardly see, the wind was whipping the snow into my face so, but a man grabbed me by the shoulder, swung me around, and shouted, "Keep moving! Keep moving! Over that way."

I headed the way he pointed. There was another man at the edge of the blast clearing, singing the same song, and there was a path through the snow, trampled to slush. I could see some other people disappearing in the snow ahead and I took out after them, dogtrotting to keep warm.

It must have been half a mile to the shelter and cold all the way. We weren't dressed for it. I was chilled through and my feet were soaking wet by the time we got inside.

The shelter was a big hangarlike building and it was not much warmer, the door was open so much, but it was out of the weather and it felt good to be inside. It was jammed with people, some of them in ship suits and some of them Ganymedeans—you couldn't miss the colonial men; they were bearded and some of them wore their hair long as well. I decided that was one style I was not going to copy; I'd be smooth shaven, like George.

I went scouting around, trying to find George & Co. I finally did. He had found a bale of something for Molly to sit on and she was holding Peggy on her lap. Peg's nose had stopped bleeding. I was glad to see, but there were dried tears and blood and dirt on her face. She was a sight.

George was looking gloomy, the way he did the first few days without his pipe. I came up and said, "Hi, folks!"

George looked around and smiled and said, "Well, Bill, fancy meeting you here! How is it going?"

"Now that you ask me," I answered, "it looks like a shambles."

He looked gloomy again and said, "Oh, I suppose they will get things straightened out presently."

We didn't get a chance to discuss it. A colonist with snow on his boots and hair on his face stopped near us, put his little fingers to his lips, and whistled. "Pipe down!" he shouted. "I want twelve able-bodied men and boys for the baggage party." He looked around and started pointing. "You—and you—and you——"

George was the ninth "You"; I was the tenth.

Molly started to protest. I think George might have balked if she had not. Instead he said, "No, Molly, I guess it has to be done. Come on, Bill."

So we went back out into the cold.

There was a tractor truck outside and we were loaded in it standing up, then we lumbered back to the rocket site. Dad saw to it that I was sent up into the *Jitterbug* to get me out of the weather and I was treated to another dose of Captain Hattie's tongue; we couldn't work fast enough to suit her. But we got our baggage lowered finally; it was in the truck by the time I was down out of the ship. The trip back was cold, too.

Molly and Peggy were not where we had left them. The big room was almost empty and we were told to go on into another building through a connecting door. George was upset, I could see, from finding Molly gone.

In the next building there were big signs with arrows: MEN & BOYS—TO THE RIGHT and WOMEN & GIRLS—TO THE LEFT. George promptly turned to the left. He got about ten yards and was stopped by a stern-faced woman dressed like a colonial, in a coverall. "Back the other way," she said firmly. "This is the way to the ladies' dormitory."

"Yes, I know," agreed Dad, "but I want to find my wife."

"You can look for her at supper."

"I want to see her *now*."

"I haven't any facilities for seeking out any one person at this time. You'll have to wait."

"But—" There were several women crowding past us and going on inside. Dad spotted one from our deck in the *Mayflower*. "Mrs. Archibald!"

She turned around. "Oh—Mr. Lermer. How do you do?"

"Mrs. Archibald," Dad said intently, "could you find Molly and let her know that I'm waiting here?"

"Why, I'd be glad to try, Mr. Lermer."

"Thanks, Mrs. Archibald, a thousand thanks!"

"Not at all." She went away and we waited, ignoring the stern-faced guard. Presently Molly showed up without Peggy. You would have thought Dad hadn't seen her for a month.

"I didn't know what to do, dear," she said. "They said we had to come and it seemed better to get Peggy settled down. I knew you would find us."

"Where is Peggy now?"

"I put her to bed."

We went back to the main hall. There was a desk there with a man behind it; over his head was a sign: IMMIGRATION SERVICE—INFORMATION. There was quite a line up at it; we took our place in the queue.

"How is Peggy?" Dad asked.

"I'm afraid she is catching a cold."

"I hope—" Dad said. "Ah, I HOPE—*Atchoo!*"

"And so are you," Molly said accusingly.

"I don't catch cold," Dad said, wiping his eyes. "That was just a reflex."

"Hmm—" said Molly.

The line up took us past a low balcony. Two boys, my age or older, were leaning on the rail and looking us over. They were colonials and one was trying to grow a beard, but it was pretty crummy.

One turned to the other and said, "Rafe, will you look at what they are sending us these days?"

The other said, "It's sad."

The first one pointed a thumb at me and went on, "Take that one, now—the artistic type, no doubt."

The second one stared at me thoughtfully. "Is it alive?" he asked.

"Does it matter?" the first one answered.

I turned my back on them, whereupon they both laughed. I hate self-panickers.

10. The Promised Land

Mr. Saunders was ahead of us in line. He was crabbing about the weather. He said it was an outrage to expose people the way we had been. He had been with us on the working party, but he had not worked much.

The man at the desk shrugged. "The Colonial Commission set your arrival date; we had nothing to say about it. You can't expect us to postpone winter to suit your convenience."

"Somebody's going to hear about this!"

"By all means." The man at the desk handed him a form. "Next, please!" He looked at Dad and said, "What may I do for you, citizen?"

Dad explained quietly that he wanted to have his family with him. The man shook his head. "Sorry. Next case, please."

Dad didn't give up his place. "You can't separate a man and wife. We aren't slaves, nor criminals, nor animals. The Immigration Service surely has some responsibilities toward us."

The man looked bored. "This is the largest shipload we've ever had to handle. We've made the best arrangements we could. This is a frontier town, not the Astor."

"All I'm asking for is a minimum family space, as

described in the Commission's literature about Ganymede."

"Citizen, those descriptions are written back on Earth. Be patient and you will be taken care of."

"Tomorrow?"

"No, not tomorrow. A few days—or a few weeks."

Dad exploded. "Weeks, indeed! Confound it, I'll build an igloo out on the field before I'll put up with this."

"That's your privilege." The man handed Dad a sheet of paper. "If you wish to lodge a complaint, write it out on this."

Dad took it and I glanced at it. It was a printed form—and it was addressed to the Colonial Commission *back on Earth!* The man went on, "Turn it in to me any time this phase and it will be ultramicrofilmed in time to go back with the mail in the *Mayflower*."

Dad looked at it, snorted, crumpled it up, and stomped away. Molly followed him and said, "George! George! Don't be upset. We'll live through it."

Dad grinned sheepishly. "Sure we will, honey. It's the beauty of the system that gets me. Refer all complaints to the head office—half a billion miles away!"

The next day George's reflexes were making his nose run. Peggy was worse and Molly was worried about her and Dad was desperate. He went off somewhere to raise a stink about the way things were being handled.

Frankly, I didn't have it too bad. Sleeping in a dormitory is no hardship to me; I could sleep through the crack of doom. And the food was everything they had promised.

Listen to this: For breakfast we had corn cakes with syrup and real butter, little sausages, *real* ham, strawberries with cream so thick I didn't know what it was, tea, all the milk you could drink, tomato juice, honeydew melon, eggs—as many eggs as you wanted.

There was an open sugar bowl, too, but the salt shaker had a little sign on it; DON'T WASTE THE SALT.

There wasn't any coffee, which I wouldn't have noticed if George had not asked for it. There were other things missing, too, although I certainly didn't notice it at the time. No tree fruits, for example—no apples, no pears, no oranges. But who cares when you can get strawberries and watermelon and pineapples and such? There were no tree nuts, too, but there were peanuts to burn.

Anything made out of wheat flour was a luxury, but you don't miss it at first.

Lunch was choice of corn chowder or jellied consomme, cheese soufflé, fried chicken, corned beef and cabbage, hominy grits with syrup, egg plant *au gratin*, little pearl onions scalloped with cucumbers, baked stuffed tomatoes, sweet potato surprise, German-fried Irish potatoes, tossed endive, coleslaw with sour cream, pineapple and cottage cheese with lettuce. Then there was peppermint ice cream, angel berry pie, frozen egg nog, raspberry ice, and three kinds of pudding—but I didn't do too well on the desserts. I had tried to try everything, taking a little of this and a dab of that, and by the time desserts came along I was short on space. I guess I ate too much.

The cooking wasn't fancy, about like Scout camp, but the food was so good you couldn't ruin it. The service reminded me of camp, too—queueing up for servings, no table cloths, no napkins. And the dishes had to be washed; you couldn't throw them away or burn them—they were imported from Earth and worth their weight in uranium.

The first day they took the first fifty kids in the chow line and the last fifty kids to leave the mess hall and made them wash dishes. The next day they changed pace on us and took the middle group. I got stuck both times.

The first supper was mushroom soup, baked ham, roast turkey, hot corn bread with butter, jellied cold meats, creamed asparagus, mashed potatoes and giblet gravy, spinach with hard boiled egg and grated cheese, corn pudding, creamed peas and carrots, smothered lettuce and three kinds of salad. Then there was frozen custard and raisin pudding with hard sauce and Malaga and Thompson grapes and more strawberries with powdered sugar.

Besides that you could drop around to the kitchen and get a snack any time you felt like it.

I didn't go outside much the first three days. It snowed and although we were in Sun phase when we got there it was so murky that you couldn't see the Sun, much less Jupiter. Besides, we were in eclipse part of the time. It was as cold as Billy-be-switched and we still didn't have any cold weather clothes.

I was sent along with the commissary tractor once to get supplies over in town. Not that I saw much of the town—and not that Leda is much of a town, anyhow, to a person who has lived in Diego Borough—but I did see the hydroponics farms. There were three of them, big multiple sheds, named for what they grew in them, "Oahu," "Imperial Valley," and "Iowa." Nothing special about them, just the usual sort of soilless gardening. I didn't hang around because the flicker lighting they use to force the plants makes my eyes burn.

But I was interested in the tropical plants they grew in "Oahu"—I had never seen a lot of them before. I noticed that most of the plants were marked "M-G" while a few were tagged "N. T." I asked one of the gardeners; he said that "M-G" meant "mutation-Ganymede" and the other meant "normal terrestrial."

I found out later that almost everything grown on Ganymede was a special mutation adapted to Ganymede conditions.

Beyond there was another of the big multiple sheds

named "Texas"; it had real cows in it and was very interesting. Did you know a cow moves its lower jaw from side to side? And no matter what you've heard, there *is not* one teat that is especially for cream.

I hated to leave, but "Texas" shed smelled too much like a space ship. It was only a short dash through the snow to the Exchange where all of Leda's retail buying and selling takes place—big and little shops all under one roof.

I looked around, thinking I might take a present back to Peggy, seeing that she was sick. I got the shock of my life. The prices!

If I had had to buy in the Exchange the measly fifty-eight pounds of stuff they had let me bring with me, it would have cost—I'm telling the truth!—several *thousand* credits. Everything that was imported from Earth cost that kind of money. A tube of beard cream was two hundred and eighty credits.

There were items for sale made on Ganymede, hand work mostly, and they were expensive, too, though not nearly as expensive as the stuff brought up from Earth.

I crept out of that place in a hurry. As nearly as I could figure the only thing cheap on Ganymede was food.

The driver of the commissary tractor wanted to know where I had been when there was loading to do? "I should have left you behind to walk back," he groused. I didn't have a good answer so I didn't say anything.

They shut off winter soon after that. The heat trap was turned on full force, the skies cleared and it was lovely. The first view I got of the Ganymede sky was a little after dawn next Sun phase. The heat trap made the sky a pale green but Jupiter shone right through it, ruddy orange, and *big*. Big and beautiful—I've never gotten tired of looking at Jupiter!

A harvest moon looks big, doesn't it? Well, Jupiter

from Ganymede is sixteen or seventeen times as wide as the Moon looks and it covers better than two hundred and fifty times as much sky. It hangs there in the sky, never rising, never setting, and you wonder what holds it up.

I saw it first in half-moon phase and I didn't see how it could be any more beautiful than it was. But the Sun crept across the sky and a day later Jupiter was a crescent and better than ever. At the middle of Sun phase we went into eclipse, of course, and Jupiter was a great red, glowing ring in the sky, brightest where the Sun had just passed behind it.

But the best of all is during dark phase.

Maybe I ought to explain how the phases work; I know I didn't understand it until I came to Ganymede. Ganymede is such a small planet and so close to its primary that it is tide-locked, just the way the Moon is; it keeps one face always toward Jupiter and therefore Jupiter does not move in the sky. The sun moves, the other Jovian moons move, the stars move—but not good old Jove; it just hangs there.

Ganymede takes just over an Earth week to revolve around Jupiter, so we have three and a half days of sunlight and then three and a half days of darkness. By Ganymede time the period of rotation is *exactly* one week; twenty-four Ganymede hours is one seventh of the period. This arrangement makes a Ganymede minute about a standard second longer than an Earth minute, but who cares? Except scientists, of course, and they have clocks that keep both sorts of time.

So here is the way a week goes on Ganymede: the Sun rises at Sunday midnight every week; when you get up Monday morning it's a little above the eastern horizon and Jupiter is in half-moon phase. The Sun keeps climbing higher and about suppertime on Tuesday it slides behind Jupiter and Ganymede is in eclipse; eclipse can last an hour or so up to a maximum of about three hours and a half. The stars come out and Jupiter shows that beautiful red ring effect because of its thick atmosphere. Then it's light again by bedtime Tuesday.

At noon on Thursday the Sun goes down and we start the dark phase; that's best of all. Jupiter's colors really show and the other moons are easier to see. They can be almost anywhere and in almost any combination.

Jupiter and its satellites is sort of a miniature solar system; from Ganymede you have a front seat for the show. There is always something new in the sky. Besides the eleven "historical" satellites ranging in size from Ganymede down to Jay-ten or Nicholson-Alpha, which is a ball of rock and ice only fifteen miles thick, there are maybe a dozen more a few miles or less in diameter but big enough to be called moons and heaven knows how many smaller than that. Sometimes these little ones come close enough to Ganymede to show discs; they mostly have very eccentric orbits. Any time there will be several that are conspicuous lights in the sky, like the planets are from Earth.

Io, and Europa, and Callisto are always discs. When Europa passes between Jupiter and Ganymede it is as big in the sky as the Moon is from Earth. It actually is as big as the Moon and at that time it is only about a quarter of a million miles away.

Then it swings around to the far side and is very much smaller—more than a million miles away and less than a quarter as wide. Io goes through the same sorts of changes, but it never gets as big.

When Io and Europa pass between Ganymede and Jupiter you can see them move with your naked eye, chasing their shadows or running ahead of them, depending on the phase. Io and Europa, being inside Ganymede's orbit, never get very far away from Jupiter. Io sticks within a couple of diameters of the big boy; Europa can get about sixty degrees away from it. Callisto is further out than Ganymede and goes all around the sky.

It's a show you never get tired of. Earth's sky is *dull*.

By six o'clock Saturday morning Jupiter would be in full phase and it was worthwhile to get up to see it. Not only was it the most gorgeous thing I had ever seen, but there was always the reverse eclipse, too, and you could see Ganymede's shadow, a little round black dot, crawling across old Jupiter's face. It gave you an idea of just how colossally *big* Jupiter was— there was the shadow of your whole planet on it and it wasn't anything more than a big freckle.

Jupiter is ninety thousand miles across the equator, eighty-four thousand from pole to pole. Ganymede is only a little better than three thousand.

For the next couple of days after full phase Jupiter would wane and at Sunday midnight it would be in half phase again, the Sun would rise and a new light phase would start. One thing I expected but didn't find was dim sunlight. Jupiter is a long way out; it gets only one twenty-seventh the sunlight that Earth does. I expected that we would always be in a sort of twilight.

It didn't work out that way. It seemed to me that the sunlight was just as bright as on Earth.

George says that this is an optical illusion and that it has to do with the way the human eye works, because the iris of the eye simply shuts out light it doesn't need. Bright desert sunlight back on Earth is maybe ten thousand foot-candles; the same thing on Ganymede is only four hundred foot-candles. But really good bright artificial light is only *twenty-five* foot candles and a "well-lighted" room is seldom that bright.

If you've got only a two-gallon bucket does it make any difference whether you fill it from the ocean or from a small pond? Sunlight on Ganymede was still more than the eye could accept, so it looked just as bright as sunlight on Earth.

I did notice, however, that it was almost impossible to get a sunburn.

11. "Share Croppers"

George got us a place to live when we had been there about a week, which was a lot better than most of the other immigrants did, but it didn't suit him and it didn't suit Molly and it didn't really suit me.

The trouble was he had to take a job as a staff engineer with the colonial government to get quarters for us—and that meant he would be too tied down to prove a piece of land for homestead. But it did carry private family quarters with it, if you could call two rooms twelve feet square a home.

It was like this: the colony was made up of homesteaders and townies. The townies worked for the government and lived in government-owned buildings —except for a very few who were in private trade. The townies included the Colonial Commission representative, Captain Hattie the pilot, the hydroponics engineers, the hospital staff, the engineers who ran the power plant and the heat trap, the staff of the local office of Project Jove, and everybody else who worked at anything but land farming. But most of the colonials were homesteaders and that's what George had meant us to be. Like most everybody, we had come out there on the promise of free land and a chance to raise our own food.

There was free land, all right, a whole planet of it. Putting up a house and proving a farm was another matter.

Here is the way it was supposed to work: A colonist comes out from Earth with his family and lands at Leda. The Colonial Commission gives him an apartment in town on arrival, helps him pick out a piece of land to improve and helps him get a house up on it. The Commission will feed him and his family for one Earth year—that is, two Ganymede years—while he gets a couple of acres under cultivation. Then he has ten G-years in which to pay back the Commission by processing at least twenty acres for the Commission— and he is allowed to process as much land for himself as for the Commission during the time he is paying what he owes. At the end of five Earth years he owns a tidy little farm, free and clear. After that, he can spread out and acquire more land, get into trade, anything he likes. He has his toehold and has paid off his debt.

The Colonial Commission had a big expensive investment in having started the atmosphere project and made the planet fit to live on in the first place. The land processed by the colonists was its return on the investment; the day would come when the Colonial Commission would own thousands of acres of prime farmland on Ganymede which it could then sell Earthside to later settlers . . . if you wanted to emigrate from Earth you would have to pay for the privilege and pay high. People like us would not be able to afford it.

By that time, although Ganymede would be closed to free immigration, Callisto would have an atmosphere and pioneers could move in there and do it all over again. It was what the bankers call "Self-liquidating," with the original investment coming from Earth.

But here is the way it actually did work out: when we landed there were only about thirty thousand people on Ganymede and they were geared to accept about five hundred immigrants an Earth year, which was about all the old-type ships could bring out. Remember, those power-pile ships took over five years for the round trip; it took a fleet of them to bring in that many a year.

Then the *Star Rover II* was renamed the *Mayflower* and turned over to the Colonial Commission, whereupon six thousand people were dumped on them all at once. We were about as welcome as unexpected overnight guests when there is sickness in the family.

The colonists had known, for a full Earth year, that we were coming, but they had not been able to protest. While Earth Sender can punch a message through to Ganymede anytime except when the Sun is spang in the way, at that time the best radio the colony could boast had to relay via Mars to reach Earth—and then only when Mars was at its closest approach to Jupiter— which it wasn't.

I've got to admit that they did what they could for us. There was plenty to eat and they had managed to fix up places for us to sleep. The Immigrants' Receiving Station had formerly been split up into family apartments; they had torn out the partitions and used the partitions to build bunks for the big dormitories we were stacked in. They had moved their town hall and made it over into a mess hall and kitchen for us. We were in out of the weather and well fed, even if we were about as crowded as we had been in the *Mayflower*.

You may ask why, with a year to get ready, they had not built new buildings for us? Well, we asked the same thing, only we weren't asking, we were demanding, and we were sore about it!

They hadn't built new buildings because they could not. Before the Earthmen moved in, Ganymede was bare rock and ice. Sure, everybody knows that—but does everybody know what that means? I'm sure I didn't.

No lumber. No sheet metal. No insulation. No wires. No glass. No pipe. The settlers in North America built log cabins—no logs.

The big hydroponics sheds, the Receiving Station and a few other public buildings had been built with materials lifted a half a billion miles from Earth. The rest of Leda and every homesteader's farm house had been built the hard way, from country rock. They had done their best for us, with what they had.

Only we didn't appreciate it.

Of course we should not have complained. After all, as George pointed out, the first California settlers starved, nobody knows what happened to the Roanoke Colony, and the first two expeditions to Venus died to the last man. *We* were safe.

Anyhow, even if we had to put up with barracks for a while, there was all that free land, waiting for us.

On close inspection, it looked as if it would have to wait quite a while. That was why George had given in and taken a staff engineering job. The closest land to town open to homesteading was nine miles away. To find enough land for six thousand people meant that most of them would have to go about eighteen to twenty miles away.

"What's twenty miles? A few minutes by tube, an up-and-down hop for a copter—brother, have you ever *walked* twenty miles? And then walked back again?

It wasn't impossible to settle six thousand people that far from town; it was just difficult—and slow. The pioneer explorer used to set out with his gun and an axe; the settler followed by hitching his oxen to a wagonload of furniture and farm tools. Twenty miles meant nothing to them.

They weren't on Ganymede.

The colony had two tractor trucks; another had come in the *Mayflower*. That's all the transportation there was on the whole planet—not just to settle six thousand people but for the daily needs of thirty thousand people who were there ahead of us.

They explained it all to us at a big meeting of heads of families. I wasn't supposed to be there but it was held outdoors and there was nothing to stop me. The chief ecologist and the chief engineer of the planet were there and the chairman of the colony council presided. Here was the proposition:

What Ganymede really needed was not more farmers, but manufacturing. They needed prospectors and mines and mills and machine shops. They needed all the things you can make out of metal and which they simply could not afford to import from Earth. That's what they wanted us to work on and they would feed any of us who accepted, not just for a year, but indefinitely.

As for any who insisted on homesteading—well, the land was there; help ourselves. There wasn't enough processing machinery to go around, so it might be two or three years before any particular immigrant got a chance to process his first acre of ground.

Somebody stood up near the front of the crowd and yelled, "We've been swindled!"

It took Mr. Tolley, the chairman, quite a while to calm them down. When they let him talk again, he said, "Maybe you have been swindled, maybe you haven't. That's a matter of opinion. I'm quite willing to concede that conditions here are not the way they were represented to you when you left Earth. In fact——"

Somebody yelled. "That's mighty nice of you!" only the tone was sarcastic.

Mr. Tolley looked vexed. "You folks can either keep order, or I'll adjourn this meeting."

They shut up again and he went on. Most of the present homesteaders had processed more land than they could cultivate. They could use hired hands to raise more crops. There was a job waiting for every man, a job that would keep him busy and teach him

Ganymede farming—and feed his wife and family—while he was waiting his turn to homestead.

You could feel a chill rolling over the crowd when the meaning of Mr. Tolley's words sunk in. They felt the way Jacob did when he had labored seven years and then was told he would have to labor another seven years to get the girl he really wanted. I felt it myself, even though George had already decided on the staff job.

A man spoke up. "Mr. Chairman!"

"Yes? Your name, please."

"Name of Saunders. I don't know how the rest of them feel, but I'm a farmer. Always have been. But I said 'farmer,' not sharecropper. I didn't come here to hire out to no boss. You can take your job and do what you see fit with it. I stand on my rights!"

There was scattered applause and the crowd began to perk up. Mr. Tolley looked at him and said, "That's your privilege, Mr. Saunders."

"Huh? Well, I'm glad you feel that way, Mr. Chairman. Now let's cut out the nonsense. I want to know two things: what piece of land am I going to get and when do I lay hands on some machinery to start putting it into condition?"

Mr. Tolley said, "You can consult the land office about your first question. As to the second, you heard the chief engineer say that he estimates the average wait for processing machinery will be around twenty-one months."

"That's too long."

"So it is, Mr. Saunders."

"Well, what do you propose to do about it?"

Mr. Tolley shrugged and spread his hands. "I'm not a magician. We've asked the Colonial Commission by urgent message going back on the *Mayflower* not to send us any more colonists on the next trip, but to send us machinery. If they agree, there may be some relief from the situation by next winter. But you have seen—all of you have already seen—that the Colonial

Commission makes decisions without consulting us. The first trip of the *Mayflower* should have been all cargo; you folks should have waited."

Saunders thought about it. "Next winter, eh? That's five months away. I guess I can wait—I'm a reasonable man. But no sharecropping; that's out!"

"I didn't say you could start homesteading in five months, Mr. Saunders. It may be twenty-one months or longer."

"No, indeedy!"

"Suit yourself. But you are confronted with a fact, not a theory. If you do have to wait and you won't work for another farmer, how do you propose to feed yourself and your family in the mean time?"

Mr. Saunders looked around and grinned, "Why, in that case, Mr. Chairman, I guess the government will just have to feed us until the government can come through on its end of the deal. I know my rights."

Mr. Tolley looked at him as if he had just bitten into an apple and found Saunders inside. "We won't let your children starve," he said slowly, "but as for you, you can go chew rocks. If you won't work, you won't eat."

Saunders tried to bluster. "You can't get away with it! I'll sue the government and I'll sue you as the responsible government official. You can't——"

"*Shut up!*" Mr. Tolley went on more quietly, speaking to all of us. "We might as well get this point straight. You people have been enticed into coming out here by rosy promises and you are understandably disappointed. But your contract is with the Colonial Commission *back on Earth*. But you have no contract with the common council of Ganymede, of which I am chairman, and the citizens of Ganymede owe you nothing. We are trying to take care of you out of common decency.

"If you don't like what we offer you, don't start throwing your weight around with me; I won't stand for it. Take it up with the representative of the Immigration Service. That's what he is here for. Meeting's adjourned!"

But the immigration representative wasn't there; he had stayed away from the meeting.

12. Bees and Zeroes

We had been swindled all right. It was equally clear that there was no help for it. Some of the immigrants did see the Colonial Commission representative, but they got no comfort out of him. He had resigned, he said, fed up with trying to carry out impossible instructions five hundred million miles from the home office. He was going home as soon as his relief arrived.

That set them off again; if he could go home so could they. The *Mayflower* was still in orbit over us, taking on cargo. A lot of people demanded to go back in her.

Captain Harkness said no, he had no authority to let them deadhead half way across the system. So they landed back on the Commission representative, squawking louder than ever.

Mr. Tolley and the council finally settled it. Ganymede wanted no soreheads, no weak sisters. If the Commission refused to ship back those who claimed they were gypped and didn't want to stay, then the next shipload wouldn't even be allowed to land. The representative gave in and wrote Captain Harkness out a warrant for their passage.

We held a family powwow over the matter, in Peggy's room in the hospital—it had to be there because the doctors were keeping her in a room pressurized to Earth normal.

Did we stay, or did we go back? Dad was stuck in a rut. Back Earthside he at least had been working for himself; here he was just an employee. If he quit his job and elected to homestead, it meant working two or three G-years as a field hand before we could expect to start homesteading.

But the real rub was Peggy. In spite of having passed her physical examination Earthside she hadn't adjusted to Ganymede's low pressure. "We might as well face it," George said to Molly. "We've got to get Peg back to the conditions she's used to."

Molly looked at him; his face was as long as my arm. "George, you don't want to go back, do you?"

"That's not the point, Molly. The welfare of the kids comes first." He turned to me and added, "You're not bound by this, Bill. You are big enough to make up your own mind. If you want to stay, I am sure it can be arranged."

I didn't answer right away. I had come into the family get-together pretty disgusted myself, not only because of the run-around we had gotten, but also because of a run-in I had had with a couple of the Colonial kids. But you know what it was that swung me around? That pressurized room. I had gotten used to low pressure and I liked it. Peggy's room, pressurized to Earth normal, felt like swimming in warm soup. I could hardly breath. "I don't think I want to go back," I said.

Peggy had been sitting up in bed, following the talk with big eyes, like a little lemur. Now she said, "I don't want to go back, either!"

Molly patted her hand and did not answer her. "George," she said, "I've given this a lot of thought. You don't want to go back, I know. Neither does Bill. But we don't all have to go back. We can——"

"That's out, Molly," Dad answered firmly. "I didn't

marry you to split up. If you have to go back, I go back."

"I didn't mean that. Peggy can go back with the O'Farrells and my sister will meet her and take care of her at the other end. She wanted me to leave Peggy with her when she found I was determined to go. It will work out all right." She didn't look at Peggy as she said it.

"But, Molly!" Dad said.

"No George," she answered, "I've thought this all out. My first duty is to you. It's not as if Peggy wouldn't be well taken care of; Phoebe will be a mother to her and——"

By now Peggy had caught her breath. "I don't *want* to go live with Aunt Phoebe!" she yelled and started to bawl.

George said, "It won't work, Molly."

Molly said, "George, not five minutes ago you were talking about leaving Bill behind, on his own."

"But Bill is practically a man!"

"He's not too old to be lonesome. And I'm not talking about leaving Peggy alone; Phoebe will give her loving care. No, George, if the womenfolk ran home at the first sign of trouble there never would be any pioneers. Peggy has to go back, but I stay."

Peggy stopped her blubbering long enough to say, "I *won't* go back! I'm a pioneer, too—ain't I, Bill?"

I said, "Sure kid, sure!" and went over and patted her hand. She grabbed onto mine.

I don't know what made me say what I did then. Goodness knows the brat had never been anything but a headache, with her endless questions and her insistence that she be allowed to do anything I did. But I heard myself saying, "Don't worry, Peggy. If you go back, I'll go with you."

Dad looked at me sharply, then turned to Peggy. "Bill spoke hastily, Baby. You mustn't hold him to that."

Peggy said, "You did so mean it, didn't you, Bill?"

I was regretting it already. But I said, "Sure, Peggy."

Peggy turned back to Dad. "See? But it doesn't matter; we're not going back, not any of us. Please Daddy —I'll get well, I promise you I will. I'm getting better every day."

Sure, she was—in a pressurized room. I sat there, sweating, and wishing I had kept my big mouth shut. Molly said, "It defeats me, George. What do you think?"

"Mmmm——"

"Well?"

"Uh, I was thinking we could pressurize one room in our quarters. I could rig some sort of an impeller in the machine shop."

Peggy was suddenly all over her tears. "You mean I can get out of the hospital?"

"That's the idea, Sugar, if Daddy can work it."

Molly looked dubious. "That's no answer to our problems, George."

"Maybe not." Dad stood up and squared his shoulders. "But I have decided one thing: we all go, or we'll all stay. The Lermers stand together. That's settled."

Homesteading wasn't the only thing we had been mistaken about. There was Scouting on Ganymede even if the news hadn't gotten back to Earth. There hadn't been any meetings of the *Mayflower* troops after we landed; everybody had been just too busy to think about it. Organized Scouting is fun, but sometimes there just isn't time for it.

There hadn't been any meetings of the Leda Troop, either. They used to meet in their town hall; now we had their town hall as a mess hall, leaving them out in the cold. I guess that didn't tend to make them feel chummy towards us.

I ran into this boy over in the Exchange. Just as he was passing me I noticed a little embroidered patch on his chest. It was a homemade job and not very good, but I spotted it. "Hey!" I said.

He stopped. " 'Hey' yourself! Were you yelling at me?"

"Uh, yes. You're a Scout, aren't you?"

"Certainly."

"So am I. My name's Bill Lermer. Shake." I slipped him the Scout grip.

He returned it. "Mine's Sergei Roskov." He looked me over. "You're one of the Johnny-Come-Latelies, aren't you?"

"I came over in the *Mayflower*," I admitted.

"That's what I meant. No offense— I was born Earthside, myself. So you used to be a Scout, back home. That's good. Come around to meeting and we'll sign you up again."

"I'm *still* a Scout," I objected.

"Huh? Oh, I get you—'Once a Scout, always a Scout.' Well, come around and we'll make it official."

That was a very good time for me to keep my lip zipped. But not me—oh, no! When comes the Tromp of Doom, I'll still be talking instead of listening. I said, "It's as official as it can be. I'm senior patrol leader, Baden-Powell Troop."

"Huh? You're kind of far away from your troop, aren't you?"

So I told him all about it. He listened until I was through, then said quietly, "And you laddie bucks had the nerve to call yourselves the 'Boy Scouts of Ganymede.' Anything else you would like to grab? You already have our meeting hall; maybe you'd like to sleep in our beds?"

"What do you mean?"

"Nothing." He seemed to be thinking it over. "Just a friendly warning, Bill——"

"Huh?"

"There is only one senior patrol leader around here —and you're looking right at him. Don't make any mistake about it. But come on around to meeting anyhow," he added. "You'll be welcome. We're always glad to sign up a new tenderfoot."

I went back to the Receiving Station and looked up Hank Jones and told him all about it. He looked at me admiringly. "William, old son," he said, "I've got to hand it to you. It takes real talent to louse things up that thoroughly. It's not easy."

"You think I've messed things up?"

"I hope not. Well, let's look up Doc Archibald and see what can be done."

Our troop master was holding clinic; we waited until the patients were out of the way, then went in. He said, "Are you two sick, or just looking for a ticket to gold brick?"

"Doc," I said, "we were wrong. There are so Scouts on Ganymede."

"So I know," he answered.

I said, "Huh?"

"Mr. Ginsberg and Mr. Bruhn and I have been negotiating with the senior Scout officials here to determine just how our troops will be taken into the parent organization. It's a bit complicated as there are actually more *Mayflower* Scouts than there are in the local troop. But they have jurisdiction, of course."

I said, "Oh."

"We'll have a joint meeting in a few days, after we get the rules ironed out."

I thought it over and decided I had better tell him what had happened, so I did.

He listened, not saying anything. Finally I said, "Hank seems to think I've messed things up. What do you think, Doc?"

"Mmmm——" he said. "Well, I hope he's wrong. But I think I may say you haven't helped the situation any."

I didn't know what to say. "Don't look so tragic about it," he urged. "You'll get well. Now run along and forget it. It may not make any difference."

But it did make a difference. Doc and the others

had been pitching for our troops to be recognized as properly constituted troops, with all ratings acknowledged. But after Sergei spread the word around, the regular Ganymede Scouts all squawked that we were nothing but a bunch of tenderfeet, no matter what we had been back on Earth. The place for us to start was the bottom; if we were any good, we could prove it— by tests.

It was compromised; George says things like that are always compromised. Ratings were confirmed on probation, with one G-year to make up any tests that were different. Our troops were kept intact. But there was one major change:

All patrol leaders had to be from the original Ganymede Scouts; they were transferred from the Leda troop. I had to admit the justice of it. How could *I* be a patrol leader on Ganymede when I was still so green that I didn't know northwest from next week? But it didn't set well with the other fellows who had been patrol leaders when the word got around that I was responsible for the flies in the soup.

Hank talked it over with me. "Billy my boy," he told me, "I suppose you realize that you are about as popular as ants at a picnic?"

"Who cares?" I objected.

"You care. Now is the time for all good men to perform an *auto da fé*."

"What in great blazing moons is an *auto da fé?*"

"In this case it means for you to transfer to the Leda Troop."

"Have you gone crazy? You know what those guys think of us, especially me. I'd be lucky to get away with my life."

"Which just goes to show how little you know about human nature. Sure, it would be a little rough for a while, but it's the quickest way to gain back some respect."

"Hank, you really are nuts. In that troop I really would be a tenderfoot—and how!"

"'That's just the point," Hank went on quietly. "We're all tenderfeet—only here in our own troop it doesn't show. If we stay here, we'll keep on being tenderfeet for a long time. But if we transfer, we'll be with a bunch who really know their way around—and some of it will rub off on us."

"Did you say 'we'?"

"I said 'we'."

"I catch on. You want to transfer, so you worked up this gag about how I ought to do so, so you would have company. A fine chum you are!"

He just grinned, completely unembarrassed. "Good old Bill! Hit him in the head eight or nine times and he can latch on to any idea. It won't be so bad, Bill. In precisely four months and nine days we won't be tenderfeet; we'll be old timers."

"Why the exact date?"

"Because that is the due date of the *Mayflower on* her next trip—as soon as *they* arrive *they'll* be the Johnny-Come-Latelies."

"Oh!"

Anyhow, we did it—and it was rough at first, especially on me . . . like the night they insisted that I tell them how to be a hero. Some twerp had gotten hold of the meteorite story. But the hazing wasn't too bad and Sergei put a stop to it whenever he caught them at it. After a while they got tired of it.

Sergei was so confounded noble about the whole thing that I wanted to kick him.

The only two merit badges to amount to anything that stood in the way of my getting off probation and back up to my old rating of Eagle Scout were agronomy and planetary ecology, Ganymede style. They were both tough subjects but well worth studying. On Ganymede you had to know them to stay alive, so I dug in.

Ecology is the most involved subject I ever tackled. I told George so and he said possibly politics was worse—and on second thought maybe politics was just one aspect of ecology. The dictionary says ecology is "the science of the interrelations of living organisms and their environment." That doesn't get you much, does it? It's like defining a hurricane as a movement of air.

The trouble with ecology is that you never know where to start because everything affects everything else. An unseasonal freeze in Texas can affect the price of breakfast in Alaska and that can affect the salmon catch and that can affect something else. Or take the old history book case: the English colonies took England's young bachelors and that meant old maids at home and old maids keep cats and the cats catch field mice and the field mice destroy the bumble bee nests and bumble bees are necessary to clover and cattle eat clover and cattle furnish the roast beef of old England to feed the soldiers to protect the colonies that the bachelors emigrated to, which caused the old maids.

Not very scientific, is it? I mean you have too many variables and you can't put figures to them. George says that if you can't take a measurement and write it down in figures you don't know enough about a thing to call what you are doing with it "science" and, as for him, he'll stick to straight engineering, thank you.

But there were some clear cut things about applied ecology on Ganymede which you could get your teeth into. Insects, for instance—on Ganymede, under no circumstances do you step on an insect. There were no insects on Ganymede when men first landed there. Any insects there now are there because the bionomics board planned it that way and the chief ecologist okayed the invasion. He wants that insect to stay right where it is, doing whatever it is that insects do; he wants it to wax and grow fat and raise lots of little insects.

Of course a Scout doesn't go out of his way to step on anything but black widow spiders and the like, anyhow—but it really brings it up to the top of your mind to know that stepping on an insect carries with it a stiff fine if you are caught, as well as a very pointed lecture telling you that the colony can get along very nicely without *you* but the insects are necessary.

Or take earthworms. I *know* they are worth their weight in uranium because I was buying them before I was through. A farmer can't get along without earthworms.

Introducing insects to a planet isn't as easy as it sounds. Noah had less trouble with his animals, two by two, because when the waters went away he still had a planet that was suited to his load. Ganymede isn't Earth. Take bees—we brought bees in the *Mayflower* but we didn't turn them loose; they were all in the shed called "Oahu" and likely to stay there for a smart spell. Bees need clover, or a reasonable facsimile. Clover would grow on Ganymede but our real use for clover was to fix nitrogen in the soil and thereby refresh a worn out field. We weren't planting clover yet because there wasn't any nitrogen in the air to fix—or not much.

But I am ahead of my story. This takes us into the engineering side of ecology. Ganymede was bare rock and ice before we came along, cold as could be, and no atmosphere to speak of—just traces of ammonia and methane. So the first thing to do was to give it an atmosphere men could breathe.

The material was there—ice. Apply enough power, bust up the water molecule into hydrogen and oxygen. The hydrogen goes up—naturally—and the oxygen sits on the surface where you can breathe it. That went on for more than fifty years.

Any idea how much power it takes to give a planet the size of Ganymede three pressure-pounds of oxygen all over its surface?

Three pressure-pounds per square inch means nine mass pounds, because Ganymede has only one third

the surface gravitation of Earth. That means you have
to start with nine pounds of ice for every square inch
of Ganymede—and that ice is *cold* to start with, better than two hundred degrees below zero Fahrenheit.

First you warm it to the freezing point, then you
melt it, then you dissociate the water molecule into
oxygen and hydrogen—not in the ordinary laboratory
way by electrolysis, but by extreme heat in a mass
converter. The result is three pressure pounds of oxygen and hydrogen mix for that square inch. It's not
an explosive mixture, because the hydrogen, being
light, sits on top and the boundary layer is too near
to being a vacuum to maintain burning.

But to carry out this breakdown takes power and
plenty of it—65,000 Btus for each square inch of surface, or for each nine pounds of ice, whichever way
you like it. That adds up; Ganymede may be a small
planet but it has 135,000,000,000,000,000 square inches
of surface. Multiply that by 65,000 Btus for each square
inch, then convert British thermal units to ergs and
you get:

92,500,000,000,000,000,000,000,000,000,000 ergs.

Ninety-two-and-a-half million billon *quadrillion* ergs!
That figure is such a beauty that I wrote it down in
my diary and showed it to George.

He wasn't impressed. George said that all figures
were the same size and nobody but a dimwit is impressed by strings of zeroes. He made me work out
what the figure meant in terms of mass-energy, by the
good old $E = MC^2$ formula, since mass-energy converters were used to give Ganymede its atmosphere.

By Einstein's law, one gram mass equals 9×10^{20} ergs,
so that fancy long figure works out to be 1.03×10^{11}
grams of energy, or 113,200 tons. It was ice, mostly,
that they converted into energy, some of the same
ice that was being turned into atmosphere—though
probably some country rock crept in along with the
ice. A mass converter will eat anything.

Let's say it was all ice; that amounts to a cube of ice a hundred and sixty feet on an edge. That was a number I felt I could understand.

I showed my answer to George and he still was not impressed. He said I ought to be able to understand one figure just as easily as the other, that both meant the same thing, and both figures were the same size.

Don't get the idea that Ganymede's atmosphere was made from a cube of ice 160 feet on a side; that was just the mass which had to be converted to energy to turn the trick. The mass of ice which was changed to oxygen and hydrogen would, if converted back into ice, cover the *entire planet* more than *twenty feet deep* —like the ice cap that used to cover Greenland.

George says all that proves is that there was a lot of ice on Ganymede to start with and that if we hadn't had mass converters we could never have colonized it. Sometimes I think engineers get so matter of fact that they miss a lot of the juice in life.

With three pressure-pounds of oxygen on Ganymede and the heat trap in place and the place warmed up so that blood wouldn't freeze in your veins colonists could move in and move around without wearing space suits and without living in pressure chambers. The atmosphere project didn't stop, however. In the first place, since Ganymede has a low escape speed, only 1.8 miles per second compared with Earth's 7 m/s, the new atmosphere would gradually bleed off to outer space, especially the hydrogen, and would be lost— in a million years or so. In the second place, nitrogen was needed.

We don't need nitrogen to breathe and ordinarily we don't think much about it. But it takes nitrogen to make protein—muscle. Most plants take it out of the ground; some plants, like clover and alfalfa and beans, take it out of the air as well and put it back into the ground. Ganymede's soil was rich in nitrogen; the original scanty atmosphere was partly ammonia—but the day would come when we would have to put the nitrogen back in that we were taking out. So the atmosphere project was now turned to making nitrogen.

This wasn't as simple as breaking up water; it called for converting stable isotope oxygen-16 into stable isotope nitrogen-14, an energy consuming reaction probably impossible in nature—or so the book said—and long considered theoretically impossible. I hadn't had any nucleonics beyond high school physics, so I skipped the equations. The real point was, it could be done, in the proper sort of a mass-energy converter, and Ganymede would have nitrogen in her atmosphere by the time her fields were exhausted and had to be replenished.

Carbon dioxide was no problem; there was dry ice as well as water ice on Ganymede and it had evaporated into the atmosphere long before the first homesteader staked out a claim.

Not that you can start farming with oxygen, carbon dioxide, and a stretch of land. That land was *dead*. Dead as Christopher Columbus. Bare rock, sterile, no life of any sort—and there never had been any life in it. It's a far piece from dead rock to rich, warm, black soil crawling with bacteria and earthworms, the sort of soil you have to have to make a crop.

It was the job of the homesteaders to make the soil.

See how involved it gets? Clover, bees, nitrogen, escape speed, power, plant-animal balance, gas laws, compound interest laws, meteorology—a mathematical ecologist has to think of *everything* and think of it ahead of time. Ecology is explosive; what seems like a minor and harmless invasion can change the whole balance. Everybody has heard of the English sparrow. There was the Australian jack rabbit, too, that darn near ate a continent out of house and home. And the Caribbean mongoose that killed the chickens it was supposed to protect. And the African snail that almost ruined the Pacific west coast before they found a parasite to kill it.

You take a harmless, useful insect, plant, or animal to Ganymede and neglect to bring along its natural enemies and after a couple of seasons you'll wish you had imported bubonic plague instead.

But that was the chief ecologist's worry; a farmer's job was engineering agronomy—making the soil and then growing things in it.

That meant taking whatever you came to—granite boulders melted out of the ice, frozen lava flows, pumice, sand, ancient hardrock—and busting it up into little pieces, grinding the top layers to sand, pulverizing the top few inches to flour, and finally infecting the topmost part with a bit of Mother Earth herself—then nursing what you had to keep it alive and make it spread. It wasn't easy.

But it was interesting. I forgot all about my original notion of boning up on the subject just to pass a merit badge test. I asked around and found out where I could see the various stages going on and went out and had a look for myself. I spent most of one light phase just looking.

When I got back to town I found that George had been looking for me. "Where in blazes have you been?" he wanted to know.

"Oh, just out and around," I told him, "seeing how the 'steaders do things."

He wanted to know where I had slept and how I had managed to eat? "Bill, it's all very well to study for your merit badges but that's no reason to turn into a tramp," he objected. "I guess I have neglected you lately—I'm sorry." He stopped and thought for a moment, then went on, "I think you had better enter school here. It's true they haven't much for you, but it would be better than running around at loose ends."

"George?"

"Yes, that's probably the best—huh?"

"Have you completely given up the idea of homesteading?"

Dad looked worried. "That's a hard question, Bill. I

still want us to, but with Peggy sick—it's difficult to say. But our name is still in the hat. I'll have to make up my mind before the drawing."

"Dad, I'll prove it."

"Eh?"

"You keep your job and take care of Peggy and Molly. I'll make us a farm."

13. Johnny Appleseed

The drawing of our division took place three weeks
later; the next day George and I walked out to see
what we had gotten. It was west of town out through
Kneiper's Ridge, new country to me; I had done my
exploring east of town, over toward the power plant,
where most of the proved land was located.

We passed a number of farms and some of them
looked good, several acres in cultivation, green and
lush, and many more acres already chewed level. It put
me in mind of Illinois, but there was something missing. I finally figured out what it was—no trees.

Even without trees it was beautiful country. On the
right, north of us, were the foothills of the Big Rock
Candy Mountains. Snow-covered peaks thrust up beyond them, twenty or thirty miles away. On the left,
curving in from the south and closer than it came to
Leda, was Laguna Serenidad. We were a couple of
hundred feet higher than the lake. It was a clear day
and I tried to see the far shore, but I couldn't be sure.

It was a mighty cheerful scene. Dad felt it, too. He
strode along, whistling "Beulah Land" off key. I get
my musical talent from Anne.

He broke off and said, "Bill, I envy you."

I said, "We'll all be together yet, George. I'm the

advance guard." I thought a bit and said, "George, do you know what the first thing I raise is going to be— after I get some food crops in?"

"What?"

"I'm going to import some seed and raise you some tobacco."

"Oh, no, Son!"

"Why not?" I knew he was touched by it, because he called me 'Son'. "I could do it, as well as not."

"It's a kind thought, but we'll have to stick to the main chance. By the time we can afford that, I will have forgotten how to light a pipe. Honest, I don't miss it."

We slogged along a bit further, not saying anything but feeling close together and good. Presently the road played out. Dad stopped and took his sketch map out of his pouch. "This must be about it."

The sketch showed where the road stopped, with just a dotted line to show where it would be, some day. Our farm was outlined on it, with the nearest corner about half a mile further along where the road ought to be and wasn't. By the map, the edge of our property—or what would be ours if we proved it—ran along the north side of the road about a quarter of a mile and from there back toward the foothills. It was marked "Plot 117-H-2" and had the chief engineer's stamp on it.

Dad was staring at where the road ended. There was a lava flow right across it, high as my head and rough as a hard winter in Maine. "Bill," he said, "How good an Indian are you?"

"Fair, I guess."

"We'll have to try to pace it off and hold a straight line due west."

But it was almost impossible to do it. We struggled and slipped on the lava and made detours. Lava looks soft and it isn't. Dad slipped and skinned his shin and I discovered that I had lost track of how many paces we had come. But presently we were across the flow and in a boulder field. It was loose rubble, from pieces the size of a house down to stuff no bigger than your fist—stuff dropped by the ice when it melted and formed Laguna Serenidad.

George says that Ganymede must have had a boisterous youth, covered with steam and volcanoes.

The boulder field was somewhat easier going but it was even harder to hold a straight line. After a bit Dad stopped. "Bill," he said, "do you know where we are?"

"No," I admitted, "but we aren't really lost. If we head back east we are bound to come to proved ground."

"Perhaps we had better."

"Wait a minute." There was a particularly big boulder ahead of us. I picked a way and managed to scramble to the top with nothing worse than a cut on my hand. I stood up. "I can see the road," I told Dad. "We're north of where we ought to be. And I think maybe we've come too far." I marked a spot with my eye and came down.

We worked south the amount I thought was right and then headed east again. After a bit I said, "I guess we missed it, George. I'm not much of an Indian."

He said, "So? What's this?" He was a little ahead of me and had stopped.

It was a cairn with a flat rock on top. Painted on it was: "117-H-2, SE corner."

We had been on our farm for the past half hour; the big boulder I had climbed up on was on it.

We sat down on a fairly flat rock and looked around. Neither of us said anything for a while; we were both thinking the same thing: if this was a farm, I was my own great uncle.

After a bit Dad muttered something. I said, "What did you say?"

"Golgotha," he said out loud. "Golgotha, the place of skulls." He was staring straight ahead.

I looked where he was looking; there was a boulder sitting on top of another and the way the sun caught it, it *did* look like a skull. It leered at us.

It was so darn quiet you could hear your hair grow. The place was depressing me. I would have given anything to hear something or see something move. Anything—just a lizard darting out from behind a rock, and I could have kissed it.

But there were no lizards here and never had been.

Presently Dad said, "Bill, are you sure you want to tackle this?"

"Sure I'm sure."

"You don't have to, you know. If you want to go back to Earth and go to M.I.T., I could arrange it for the next trip."

Maybe he was thinking that if I went back, I could take Peggy with me and she would be willing to go. Maybe I should have said something about it. But didn't; I said, "Are you going back?"

"No."

"Neither am I." At the moment is was mostly stubbornness. I had to admit that our "farm" wasn't flowing with milk and honey; in fact it looked grim. Nobody but a crazy hermit would want to settle down in such a spot.

"Think it over, Bill."

"I've thought it over."

We sat there a while longer, not saying anything, just thinking long thoughts. Suddenly we were almost startled out of our boots by somebody yodelling at us. A moment before I had been wishing to hear just anything, but when it came it was like unexpectedly encountering a clammy hand in the dark.

We both jumped and Dad said, "What in the——?" I looked around. There was a large man coming toward us. In spite of his size he skipped through the rocks like a mountain goat, almost floating in the low gravity. As he got closer I knew I had seen him before; he was on the Court of Honor, a Mr. Schultz.

Dad waved to him and pretty soon he reached us. He stood half a head taller than Dad and would have made the pair of us, he was so big. His chest was as thick as my shoulders were broad and his belly was thicker than that. He had bushy, curly red hair and his beard spread out over his chest like a tangle of copper springs. "Greetings, citizens," he boomed at us, "my name is Johann Schultz."

Dad introduced us and he shook hands and I almost lost mine in his. He fixed his eyes on me and said, "I've seen you before, Bill."

I said I guessed he had, at Scout meetings. He nodded and added, "A patrol leader, no?"

I admitted that I used to be. He said, "And soon again," as if the matter were all settled. He turned to Dad. "One of the kinder saw you going past on the road, so Mama sent me to find you and bring you back to the house for tea and some of her good coffee cake."

Dad said that was very kind but that we didn't want to impose. Mr. Schultz didn't seem to hear him. Dad explained what we were there for and showed him the map and pointed out the cairn. Mr. Schultz nodded four or five times and said, "So we are to be neighbors. Good, good!" He added to Dad "My neighbors call me John, or sometimes 'Johnny'." Dad said his name was George and from then on they were old friends.

Mr. Schultz stood by the cairn and sighted off to the west and then north to the mountains. Then he scrambled up on a big boulder where he could see better and looked again. We went up after him.

He pointed to a rise west of us. "You put your house so, not too far from the road, but not on it. And first you work this piece in here and next season you work back further toward the hills." He looked at me and added. "No?"

I said I guessed so. He said, "It is good land, Bill. You will make a fine farm." He reached down and picked up a piece of rock and rubbed it between his fingers. "Good land," he repeated.

He laid it down carefully, straightened up, and said, "Mama will be waiting for us."

Mama was waiting for us, all right, and her idea of a piece of coffee cake was roughly what they used to welcome back the Prodigal Son. But before we got into the house we had to stop and admire the Tree.

It was a real tree, an apple tree, growing in a fine bluegrass lawn out in front of his house. Furthermore it was bearing fruit on two of its limbs. I stopped and stared at it.

"A beauty, eh, Bill?" Mr. Schultz said, and I agreed. "Yes," he went on, "it's the most beautiful tree on Ganymede—you know why? Because it's the *only* tree on Ganymede." He laughed uproariously and dug me in the ribs as if he had said something funny. My ribs were sore for a week.

He explained to Dad all the things he had had to do to persuade it to grow and how deep down he had had to go to prepare for it and how he had had to channel out to drain it. Dad asked why it was bearing only on one side. "Next year we pollenate the other side," he answered, "and then we have Stark's Delicious. And Rome Beauties. This year, Rhode Island Greenings and Winesaps." He reached up and picked one. "A Winesap for you, Bill."

I said thanks and bit into it. I don't know when I've tasted anything so good.

We went inside and met Mama Schultz and four or five other Schultzes of assorted sizes, from a baby crawling around in the sand on the floor up to a girl as old as I was and nearly as big. Her name was Gretchen and her hair was red like her father's, only it was straight and she wore it in long braids. The boys were mostly blond, including the ones I met later.

The house was mainly a big living room, with a big table down the middle of it. It was a solid slab of rock, maybe four feet wide and twelve or thirteen feet long, supported by three rock pillars. A good thing it was rock, the way Mama Schultz loaded it down.

There were rock slab benches down the long sides and two real chairs, one at each end, made out of oil drums and padded with stuffed leather cushions.

Mama Schultz wiped her face and hands on her apron and shook hands and insisted that Dad sit down in her chair; she wouln't be sitting down much, she explained. Then she turned back to her cooking while Gretchen poured tea for us.

The end of the room was the kitchen and was centered around a big stone fireplace. It had all the earmarks of being a practical fireplace—and it was, as I found out later, though of course nothing had ever been burned in it. It was really just a ventilation hole. But Papa Schultz had wanted a fireplace so he had a fireplace. Mama Schultz's oven was set in the side of it.

It was faced with what appeared to be Dutch tile, though I couldn't believe it. I mean, who is going to import anything as useless as ornamental tile all the way from Earth? Papa Schultz saw me looking at them and said, "My little girl Kathy paints good, huh?" One of the medium-sized girls blushed and giggled and left the room.

I had the apple down to a very skinny core and was wondering what to do with it in that spotless room when Papa Schultz stuck out his hand. "Give it to me, Bill."

I did. He took out his knife and very gently separated out the seeds. One of the kids left the room and fetched him a tiny paper envelope in which he placed the seeds and then sealed it. He handed it to me. "There, Bill," he said. "I have only one apple tree, but you have eight!"

I was sort of surprised, but I thanked him. He went on, "That place just this side of where you will build your house—if you will fill that gully from the bottom, layer by layer, building your soil as you go, with only a very little 'pay dirt' you will have a place that will support a whole row of trees. When your seedlings are big, we'll bud from my tree."

I put them very carefully in my pouch.

Some of the boys drifted in and washed up and soon we were all sitting around the table and digging into fried chicken and mashed potatoes and tomato preserves and things. Mama Schultz sat beside me and kept pressing food on me and insisting that I wasn't eating enough to keep body and soul together which wasn't true.

Afterwards I got acquainted with the kids while George and Papa Schultz talked. Four of the boys I knew; they were Scouts. The fifth boy, Johann junior —they called him "Yo"—was older than I, almost twenty, and worked in town for the chief engineer. The others were Hugo and Peter, both Cubs, then Sam, and then Vic, who was an Explorer Scout, same as I was. The girls were the baby, Kathy and Anna, who seemed to be twins but weren't, and Gretchen. They all talked at once.

Presently Dad called me over. "Bill, you know we don't rate a chance at a rock crusher for several months."

"Yes," I said, somewhat mystified.

"What are your plans in the meantime?"

"Uh, well, I don't know exactly. Study up on what I'll have to do."

"Mmm . . . Mr. Schultz has very kindly offered to take you on as a farm hand in the meantime. What do you think of the idea?"

14. Land of My Own

Papa Schultz needed a field hand about as much as I need four ears, but that didn't keep me from moving in. In that family everybody worked but the baby and you could count on it that she would be washing dishes as soon as she was up off the floor. Everybody worked all the time and seemed to enjoy it. When the kids weren't working they were doing lessons and the boys were punished when they weren't up on their lessons by being required to stay in from the fields.

Mama would listen to them recite while she cooked. Sometimes she listened to lessons in things I'm pretty sure she never had studied herself, but Papa Schultz checked up on them, too, so it didn't matter.

Me, I learned about pigs. And cows. And chickens. And how you breed pay dirt to make more pay dirt. "Pay dirt" is the stuff that is actually imported from Earth, concentrated soil cultures with the bacteria and so forth in it you have to have to get a field alive.

There was an awful lot to learn. Take cows, now—half the people you meet can't tell their left hands from their right so who would think that a cow would care about such things? But they do, as I found out when I tried to milk one from the left.

Everything was stoop labor around the place, as

primitive as a Chinese farm. The standard means of transportation was a wheelbarrow.

I learned not to sneer at a wheelbarrow after I priced one at the Exchange.

The total lack of power machinery wasn't through lack of power; the antenna on the farm house roof could pick up as much power as necessary—but there wasn't any machinery. The only power machinery in the colony belonged to the whole colony and was the sort of thing the colony absolutely couldn't get along without, like rock chewers and the equipment for the heat trap and the power plant itself.

George explained it this way: every load that was sent up from Earth was a compromise between people and cargo. The colonists were always yapping for more machinery and fewer immigrants; the Colonial Commission always insisted on sending as many people as possible and holding the imports down to a minimum.

"The Commission is right, of course," he went on. "If we have people, we'll get machinery—we'll make it ourselves. By the time you have a family of your own, Bill, immigrants will arrive here bare-handed, no cargo at all, and we'll be able to outfit a man with everything from plastic dishes for his cupboard to power cultivators for his fields."

I said, "If they wait until I have a family, they'll have a long wait. I figure a bachelor travels faster and further."

Dad just grinned, as if he knew something I didn't know and wouldn't tell. I had walked into town to have dinner with him and Molly and the kid. I hadn't seen much of them since I went to work for Papa Schultz. Molly was teaching school, Peggy couldn't come out to the farm, of course, and Dad was very busy and very excited over a strike of aluminum oxides twenty miles east of town. He was in the project up to his ears and talking about having sheet aluminum on sale in another G-year.

As a matter of fact, cultivating a farm by stoop labor wasn't too bad, not on Ganymede. Low gravity was a big help; you didn't wear yourself out just dragging your own carcass around. I grossed a hundred and forty-two mass pounds, what with the way Mama Schultz stuffed me; that meant I weighed less than fifty pounds, field boots and all. A wheelbarrow was similarly light when loaded.

But the real advantage that made the work easy was something you might not guess.

No weeds.

No weeds at all; we had very carefully not imported any. Once the land was built, making a crop was darn near a case of poking a seed into the ground and then stepping back quick before the stalk shot up and hit you in the eye.

Not that we didn't work. There is plenty of work around a farm even with no weeds to worry about. And a light wheelbarrow load simply meant that we piled three times as much on. But we had fun, too; I never met a family that laughed so much.

I brought my squeeze box out from town and used to play it after supper. We would all sing, with Papa Schultz booming away on his own and leaving it up to the rest of us to find the key he was singing in. We had fun.

It turned out that Gretchen was an awful tease when she got over being shy. But I could always get her goat by pretending that her head was on fire and either warming my hands over her hair or threatening to pour water on her before she burned the place down.

The day finally came when it was my turn to have the colony's crushers work on my land and I was almost sorry to see it arrive; I had had such a nice time at the Schultz's. But by then I could caponize a rooster or plant a row of corn; I still had a lot to learn, but there wasn't any good reason why I shouldn't start making my own farm.

Dad and I had had to prepare our farm for the crusher by dynamiting the biggest boulders. A crusher will choke on anything much bigger than a barrel but it will handle up to that size very nicely. Dynamite is cheap, thank goodness, and we used plenty of it. The raw material is nitroglycerine which we didn't have to import from Earth, the glycerine being refined from animal fats and the nitric acid being a synthetic byproduct of the atmosphere project.

Dad spent two weekends with me, making medium-sized ones out of big ones, then decided it was safe to trust me to set powder by myself and I finished the job. There was a little stream of melted snow water coming down from the hills at the far side of our property; we blew out a new bed for it to lead it close to the place where the house would go. We left it dry for the time being, with a natural rock dam to blow up later. One fair-sized hill we moved entirely and blew it into a gully on the lake side of the land. *Big* charges that took and I almost got fitted for a halo through underestimating how far some of the stuff would throw.

It was easy work and lots of fun. I had a vibro-drill, borrowed from the engineer's office; you could sink a charge hole with it twenty feet into rock as easily as you could sink a hot knife into butter. Then drop in the powder, fill the rest of the hole with rock dust, light the fuse, and run like the dickens!

But the most fun was blowing up that rock that looked like a grinning skull. I fixed it properly, it and its leer!

We had a visitor while we were dynamiting the land. Dad and I had just knocked off for lunch one day when Saunders, "The One-Man Lobby"—that's George's name for him—showed up. We invited him to share what we had; he had brought nothing but his appetite.

He complained about this and that. Dad tried to change the subject by asking him how he was getting along with his blasting. Saunders said it was slow work. Dad said, "You have the crusher the day after us, don't you?"

Saunders admitted it and said he wanted to borrow some powder; he was running short of time. Dad let him have it, though it meant another trip out from town, after work, for him the next day. Saunders went on, "I've been looking this situation over, Mr. Lermer. We're tackling it all wrong."

George said, "So?"

Saunders said, "Yes, indeedy! Now in the first place this blasting ought not to be done by the homesteader; it should be done by trained crews, sent out by the government. It's really part of the contract anyway; we're supposed to receive processed land."

Dad said mildly that, while that might be a nice idea, he didn't know where they would find enough trained crews to do the work for fifteen hundred new farms.

"Let the government hire them!" Mr. Saunders answered. "Bring them in from Earth for that purpose. Now, see here, Mr. Lermer, you are in the chief engineer's office. You ought to put in a word for the rest of us."

George picked up the vibro and got ready to set a charge. Presently he answered, "I'm afraid you've come to the wrong party. I'm in an entirely different department."

I guess Mr. Saunders saw he was off on the wrong tack for he went on, "In the second place, I have been looking into the matter of the soil, or what they call 'soil'—again they are off on the wrong foot." He kicked a rock. "This stuff isn't good for anything. You can't grow anything in stuff like that."

"Naturally not," agreed Dad. "You have to make soil first."

"That's just what I'm getting at," Saunders went on. "You have to have soil—good, black, rich soil. So they tell us to breed it, a square foot at a time. Plough garbage into it, raise earthworms—I don't know how many tomfool stunts."

"Do you know of a better way?"

"You bet you I do! That's just what I'm getting at. Here we are, piddling along, doing things the way a bunch of bureaucrats who never made a crop tell us to, all for a few inches of second-rate soil—when there are millions of cubic feet of the richest sort of black soil going begging."

Dad looked up sharply. "Where?"

"In the Mississippi Delta, that's where! Black soil goes down there for hundreds of feet."

We both looked at him, but he was quite serious about it. "Now here's what you've got to have—Level the ground off, yes. But after that spread real Earth soil over the rock to a depth of at least two feet; then it will be worth while to farm. As it is, we are just wasting our time."

Dad waited a bit before answering, "Have you figured out what this would cost?"

Mr. Saunders brushed that aside. "That's not the point; the point is, that's what we've got to have. The government wants us to settle here, doesn't it? Well, then, if we all stick together and insist on it, we'll get it." He jerked his chin triumphantly.

George started to say something, then stopped. He patted rock dust in on top of his charge, then straightened up and wiped the sweat off his beard. "Listen, citizen," he said, "can't you see that we are busy? I'm about to light this fuse; I suggest that you back away out of danger."

"Huh?" said Saunders. "How big a charge is it? How far?"

If he had kept his eyes open, he would have seen how big a charge it was and known how far to give back. Dad said, "Oh, say a mile and a half—or even two miles. And keep backing."

Saunders looked at him, snorted disgustedly, and stalked away. We backed out of range and let her blow.

While we were setting the next charge I could see George's lips moving. After a while he said, "Figuring gumbo mud conservatively at a hundred pounds per cubic foot it would take one full load of the *Mayflower* to give Mr. Saunders alone the kind of a farm he would like to have handed to him. At that rate it would take just an even thousand G-years—five hundred Earth years—for the *Mayflower* to truck in topsoil for farms for our entire party."

"You forgot the *Covered Wagon*," I said brightly.

George grinned. "Oh, yes! When the *Covered Wagon* is commissioned and in service we could cut it down to two hundred and fifty years—provided no new immigrants came in and there was a ban on having babies!" He frowned and added, "Bill, why is it that some apparently-grown men never learn to do simple arithmetic?" I didn't know the answer, so he said, "Come on, Bill, let's get on with our blasting. I'm afraid we'll just have to piddle along in our inefficient way, even if it doesn't suit our friend Saunders."

The morning the crusher was scheduled to show up I was waiting for it at the end of the road. It came breezing down the road at twenty miles an hour, filling it from side to side. When it came to the wall of lava, it stopped. I waved to the operator; he waved back, then the machine grunted a couple of times, inched forward, and took a bite out of the lava.

Lava didn't bother it; it treated it like peanut brittle. A vibro-cutter built into its under carriage would slice under the flow like a housewife separating biscuit from a pan, the big steel spade on the front of the thing would pry under and crack the bite off, and the conveyor would carry the chunk up into the jaws.

The driver had a choice of dropping the chewed up material under the rear rollers or throwing it off to the side. Just now he was throwing it away, leaving the clean slice made by the vibro-cutter as a road bed —a good road, a little dusty but a few rains would fix that.

It was terrifically noisy but the driver didn't seem to mind. He seemed to enjoy it; there was a good breeze taking the dust away from him and he had his anti-silicosis mask pushed up on his forehead, showing the grin on his face.

By noon he was down to our place and had turned in. We had a bite to eat together, then he started in levelling a farm for me—five acres, the rest would have to wait. At that I was lucky for I was to get land to work months ahead of the original schedule. The second trip of the *Mayflower* had brought in three more crushers and very few immigrants, just enough to replace those who had given up and gone back out of our party, that being the compromise the town council had worked out with the Colonial Commission.

The racket was still worse when the crusher bit into hard rock, instead of lava, but it was music to me and I didn't get tired of watching. Every bite was a piece of land to me. At suppertime the second-shift driver showed up with Dad. We watched together for a while, then Dad went back to town. I stayed. About midnight I went over into a stretch that was not to be processed now, found a big rock to keep the Sun out of my eyes and lay down for a quick nap.

Then the relief driver was shaking me and saying, "Wake up, kid—you got a farm."

I stood up and rubbed my eyes and looked around. Five acres, with just enough contour for drainage and a low hummock in the middle where the house would sit. I had a farm.

The next logical thing to do would have been to get the house up, but, under the schedule, I rated the use of a cud-chewer for the following week. A cud-chewer is a baby rock crusher. It uses a power pack instead of an antenna, it is almost fool proof and anybody can run one, and it finishes up what the crusher starts. It is small and low-powered compared with a crusher. The colony had about forty of them.

The crusher left loose rubble several feet deep in pieces as big as my fist. The cud-chewer had a fork spade on the front of it, several sizes of spade forks, in fact. The coarse fork went down into the loose rocks about eighteen inches and picked up the big ones. These drifted back into the hopper as the machine moved forward and were busted into stuff about the size of walnuts.

When you had been over the ground once with the coarse fork, you unshipped it and put on the medium fork and reset the chewing rollers. This time you went down only ten inches and the result was gravel. Then you did it again for medium-fine and then fine and when you were done the upper six inches or so was rock flour, fine as the best loam—still dead, but ready to be bred into life.

Round and round and round, moving forward an inch at a time. To get real use out of your time allotment the cud-chewer had to be moving twenty-four hours a day until they took it away from you. I stayed at it all through the first day, eating my lunch in the saddle. Dad spelled me after supper and Hank came out from town and we alternated through the night—light phase it was, actually, it being Monday night.

Papa Schultz found me asleep with my head on the controls late next afternoon and sent me back to his house to get some real sleep. Thereafter one of the Schultzes always showed up when I had been at it alone for four or five hours. Without the Schultzes I don't know how Dad and I would have gotten through the dark phase of that week.

But they did help and by the time I had to pass the cud-chewer along I had nearly three and a half acres ready to be seeded with pay dirt.

Winter was coming on and I had my heart set on getting my house up and living in it during the winter month, but to do so I really had to hump. I had to get some sort of a holding crop in or the spring thaw would wash my top soil away. The short Ganymede year is a good idea and I'm glad they run it that way; Earth's winters are longer than necessary. But it keeps you on the jump.

Papa Schultz advised grass; the mutated grass would grow in sterile soil much like growing things in hydroponic solutions. The mat of rootlets would hold my soil even if the winter killed it and the roots would furnish something through which the infection could spread from the "pay dirt."

Pay dirt is fundamentally just good black soil from Earth, crawling with bacteria and fungi and microscopic worms—everything you need but the big fishing worms; you have to add those. However, it wouldn't do simply to ship Earth dirt to Ganymede by the car load. In any shovelful of loam there are hundreds of things, plant and animal, you need for growing soil—but there are hundreds of other things you don't want. Tetanus germs. Plant disease viruses. Cut worms. Spores. Weed seeds. Most of them are too small to be seen with the naked eye and some of them can't even be filtered out.

So to make pay dirt the laboratory people back on Earth would make pure cultures of everything they wanted to keep in the way of bacteria, raise the little worms under laboratory conditions, do the same for fungi and everything else they wanted to save—and take the soil itself and kill it deader than Luna, irradiate it, bake it, test it for utter sterility. Then they would take what they had saved in the way of life forms and put it back into the dead soil. That was "pay dirt," the original pay dirt. Once on Ganymede the original stuff would be cut six ways, encouraged to grow, then cut again. A hundred weight of pay dirt supplied to a 'steader might contain a pound of Terra's own soil.

Every possible effort was made to "limit the invasion," as the ecologists say, to what was wanted. One thing that I may not have mentioned about the trip out was the fact that our clothes and our baggage were sterilized during the trip and that we ourselves were required to take a special scrub before we put our clothes back on. It was the only good bath I got the whole two months, but it left me smelling like a hospital.

The colony's tractor trucks delivered the pay dirt I was entitled to in order to seed my farm; I left the Schultz place early that morning to meet them. There is difference of opinion as to the best way to plant pay dirt; some 'steaders spread it all over and take a chance on it dying; some build up little pockets six or eight feet apart, checker board style . . . safe but slow. I was studying the matter, my mind not made up, when I saw something moving down the road.

It was a line of men, pushing wheelbarrows, six of them. They got closer and I could see that it was all the male Schultzes. I went out to meet them.

Every one of those wheelbarrows was loaded with garbage and all for me!

Papa Schultz had been saving it as a surprise for me. I didn't know what to say. Finally I blurted out, "Gee, Papa Schultz, I don't know when I'll be able to pay you back!"

He looked fierce and said, "Who is speaking of paying back when we have compost running out of our ears yet?" Then he had the boys dump their loads down on top of my pay dirt, took a fork and began mixing it as gently as Mama Schultz folding in beaten egg white.

He took charge and I didn't have to worry about the best way to use it. In his opinion—and you can't bet that I didn't buck it!—what we had was good for about an acre and his method was to spread it through the soil. But he did not select one compact acre; he laid out strips, seven of them, a couple of hundred yards long each and stretching across my chewed soil thirty-five or forty feet apart. Each of us took a wheelbarrow—their six and my one—and distributed the mix along each line.

When that was done and cairns had been set to show where the strips ran, we raked the stuff into the rock dust five or six feet on each side of each line. Around noon Mama and Gretchen showed up, loaded down, and we stopped and had a picnic.

After lunch Yo had to go back to town but he had almost finished his strip. Papa had finished his and proceeded to help Hugo and Peter who were too small to swing a good rake. I dug in and finished mine soon enough to be able to finish what Yo had left. Dad showed up at the end of the day, expecting to help me all evening—it was light phase and you could work as late as you could stand up under it—but there was nothing left to do. And he didn't know how to thank them either.

I like to think that we would have gotten the farm made anyhow, without the Schultzes, and maybe we would have—but I'm sure not sure. Pioneers need good neighbors.

The following week I spent working artificial nitrates from the colony's power pile into the spaces between the strips—not as good as pay dirt from Earth, but not as expensive, either.

Then I tackled sowing the grass, by hand, just like in the Bible, and then raking it gently in. That old pest Saunders showed up. He still did so every now and then, but never when Dad was around. I guess he was lonely. His family was still in town and he was camping out in a ten-foot rock shed he had built. He wasn't really making a farm, not properly; I couldn't figure out what he was up to. It didn't make sense.

I said, "Howdy," and went on with my work.

He watched me, looking sour, and finally said, "You still bent on breaking your heart on this stuff, aren't you, youngster?"

I told him I hadn't noticed any wear and tear on my pump, and anyhow, wasn't he making a farm, too?

He snorted. "Not likely!"

"Then what *are* you doing?"

"Buying my ticket, that's what."

"Huh?"

"The only thing you can sell around this place is improved land. I'm beating them at their own game, that's what. I'll get that land in shape to unload it on some other sucker and then me and mine are heading straight back for that ever-lovin' Earth. And that's just what you'll be doing if you aren't an utter fool. You'll never make a farm here. It can't be done."

I was getting very tired of him but I'm short on the sort of point-blank guts it takes to be flatly rude. "Oh, I don't know," I said. "Look at Mr. Schultz—he's got a good farm."

Saunders snorted again. "You mean 'Johnny Appleseed'?"

"I mean Mr. Johann Schultz."

"Sure, sure—Johnny Appleseed. That's what everybody calls him in town. He's nuts. You know what he did? He gave me a handful of apple seeds and acted like he had handed me the riches of Solomon."

I stopped raking. "Well, hadn't he?"

Saunders spat on the ground between us. "He's a clown."

I lifted up the head of the rake. I said, "Mr. Saunders, you are standing on my land, my property. I'll give you just two shakes to get off it and never set foot on it again!"

He backed away and said, "Hey! You stop that! Watch what you are doing with that rake!"

I said, "Git!"

He got.

The house was a problem. Ganymede has little quakes all the time. It has to do with "isostasy" which doesn't mean a thing but "equal-pressure" when you get right down to it, but it's the science of how the mountains balance the seas and the gravitation of a planet all comes out even.

It has to do with tidal strains, too, which is odd,

since Ganymede doesn't have any tides; the Sun is too far away to matter and Ganymede always keeps the same face toward Jupiter. Oh, you can detect a little tide on Laguna Serenidad when Europa is closest to Ganymede and even a trifle from Callisto and Io, but what I mean is it doesn't have *tides*—not like the Pacific Ocean.

What it does have is a frozen tidal strain. The way Mr. Hooker, the chief meteorologist, explains it is that Ganymede was closer to Jupiter when it cooled off and lost its rotation, so that there is a tidal bulge in the planet itself—sort of a fossil tidal bulge. The Moon has one, you know.

Then we came along and melted off the ice cap and gave Ganymede an atmosphere. That rearranged the pressures everywhere and the isostatic balance is readjusting. Result: little quakes all the time.

I'm a California boy; I wanted a quakeproof house. Schultzes had a quakeproof house and it seemed like a good idea, even though there had never been a quake heavy enough to knock a man down, much less knock a house down. On the other hand most of the colonists didn't bother; it is hard to make a rock house really quakeproof.

Worse than that, it's expensive. The basic list of equipment that a 'steader is promised in his emigration contract reads all right, a hoe, a spade, a shovel, a wheelbarrow, a hand cultivator, a bucket, and so forth down the list—but when you start to farming you find that is only the beginning and you've got to go to the Exchange and buy a lot of other stuff. I was already in debt a proved acre and a half, nearly, before the house ever went up.

As usual we compromised. One room had to be quake proof because it had to be air tight—Peggy's room. She was getting better all the time, but she still couldn't take low pressure for any length of time. If the family was going to move out to the farm, her bedroom had to be sealed, it had to have an air lock on it, and we had to have an impeller. All that runs into money.

Before I was through I had to pledge two more acres. Dad tried to sign for it but they told him bluntly that while a 'steader's credit was good, his wasn't. That settled the matter. We planned on one reinforced room and hoped to build on to it later. In the mean time the house would be a living room, ten by twelve, where I would sleep, a separate bedroom too small to swing a cat for George and Molly, and Peggy's room. All but Peggy's room would be dry wall rock with a patent roof.

Pretty small, eh? Well, what's wrong with that? Abe Lincoln started with less.

I started in cutting the stone as soon as the seed was in. A vibro-saw is like a vibro-drill, except that it cuts a hair line instead of drilling a hole. When the power is on you have to be durned careful not to get your fingers or anything into the field, but it makes easy work of stone cutting. By the contract you got the use of one for forty-eight hours free and another forty-eight hours, if you wanted it, at a reduced rate. I got my work lined up and managed to squeeze it into the two free days. I didn't want to run up any more debt, because there was another thing I was hankering for, come not later than the second spring away—flicker flood lights. Papa Schultz had them for his fields and they just about doubled his crops. Earth plants aren't used to three and half days of darkness, but, if you can tickle them during the dark phase with flicker lights, the old photosynthesis really gets in and humps itself.

But that would have to wait.

The patrol got the house up—the patrol I was in, I mean, the Auslanders. It was a surprise to me and yet it wasn't, because everybody has a house raising; you can't do it alone. I had already taken part in six my-

self—not just big-heartedness, don't get me wrong.
I had to learn how it was done.

But the patrol showed up before I had even passed
the word around that I was ready to hold a house raising. They came swinging down our road; Sergei
marched them up to where the house was to be, halted
them, and said to me, "Bill, are your Scout dues paid
up?" He sounded fierce.

I said, "You know they are."

"Then you can help. But don't get in our way." Suddenly he grinned and I knew I had been framed. He
turned to the patrol and shouted, "House raising drill!
Fall out and fall to."

Suddenly it looked like one of those TV comedies
where everything has been speeded up. I never saw
anybody work the way they did. Let me tell you it
doesn't take Scout uniforms to make Scouts. None
of us ever had uniforms; we couldn't afford special
clothes just for Scouting.

Besides the Auslanders there was Vic Schultz and
Hank Jones, both from the Hard Rock patrol and
Doug Okajima, who wasn't even of our troop but still
with the Baden-Powell. It did my heart good. I hadn't
seen much of the fellows lately; during light phase I
always worked too late to get in to meetings; during
dark phase a cold nine miles into town after supper
is something to think twice about.

I felt sheepish to realize that while I might have
forgotten them, they hadn't forgotten me, and I resolved to get to meetings, no matter how tired I was.
And take the tests for those two merit badges, too—the
very first chance I got.

That reminded me of another item of unfinished
business, too—Noisy Edwards. But you can't take a
day off just to hunt somebody up and poke him in
the snoot, not when you are making a farm. Besides
it wouldn't hurt anything for me to put on another ten
pounds; I didn't want it to be a repetition of the last
time.

Dad showed up almost immediately with two men from his office and he took charge of bracing and sealing Peggy's room. The fact that he showed up at all let me know that he was in on it—which he admitted. It had been Sergei's idea and that was why Dad had put me off when I said it was about time to invite the neighbors in.

I got Dad aside. "Look, George," I said, "how in nation are we going to feed 'em?"

"Don't worry about it," he said.

"But I do worry about it!" Everybody knows it's the obligation of the 'steader whose house is being raised to provide the victuals and I had been taken by surprise.

"I said not to," he repeated. And presently I knew why; Molly showed up with Mama Schultz, Gretchen, Sergei's sister Marushka, and two girls who were friends of Peggy—and what they were carrying they couldn't have carried on Earth. It was a number one picnic and Sergei had trouble getting them back to work after lunch.

Theoretically, Molly had done the cooking over at the Schultz's but I know Mama Schultz—anyhow, let's face it, Molly wasn't much of a cook.

Molly had a note for me from Peggy. It read: "Dearest Billy, Please come into town tonight and tell me all about it. Pretty please!" I told Molly I would.

By eighteen o'clock that afternoon the roof was on and we had a house. The door wasn't hung; it was still down at the 'Change. And the power unit wasn't in and might not be for a week. But we had a house that would keep off the rain, and a pint-sized cow barn as well, even if I didn't own a cow.

15. Why Did We Come?

According to my diary we moved into the house on the first day of spring.

Gretchen came over and helped me get ready for them. I suggested that we ask Marushka as well, since there would be lots of work to do. Gretchen said, "Suit yourself!" and seemed annoyed, so I didn't. Women are funny. Anyhow Gretchen is a right good worker.

I had been sleeping in the house ever since the raising and even before the technicians from the engineer's office had come and installed the antenna on the roof and rigged the lights and heat—but that was done before winter was started and I passed a comfortable month, fixing up the inside of the place and getting in a crop of ice for the summer. I stored the ice, several tons of it, in the gully at the side of the house, where I meant to plant apple trees just as soon as I could get fixed for it. The ice would keep there until I could build a proper cold cellar.

The first few months after the folks moved out are the happiest I can remember. We were together again and it was good. Dad still spent most of each dark phase in town, working on a part time basis, but that was quite as much because he was interested in the manufacturing project as it was to help pay off our debts. During light phase we worked almost around the clock, side by side or at least within earshot.

Molly seemed to like being a housewife. I taught her how to cook and she caught on real fast. Ganymede cooking is an art. Most things have to be cooked under pressure, even baked things, for water boils at just a little over a hundred and forty degrees. You can stir boiling water with your finger if you don't leave it in too long. Then Molly started learning from Mama Schultz but I didn't mind that; Mama Schultz was an artist. Molly got to be a really good cook.

Peg had to live in her room, of course, but we had hopes that she would be out soon. We had the pressure down to eight pounds, half oxygen and half nitrogen, and we usually all ate in her room. I still hated the thick stuff but it was worth while putting up with it so that the family could eat together. After a while I got so that I could change pressure without even an earache.

Peggy could come outside, too. We had brought her from town in a bubble stretcher—another thing bought on credit!—and Dad had fitted it with the gas apparatus from an old space suit he had salvaged from the Project Jove people. Peggy could get into the stretcher and shut herself in and we could bleed off the pressure in her room and take her outside where she could get some sunshine and look at the mountains and the lake and watch Dad and me work in the fields. The clear plastic of the bubble did not stop ultraviolet and it was good for her.

She was a skinny little runt and it was no trouble to move her around, even in the stretcher. Light phase, she spent a lot of time outdoors.

We had started with a broody hen and fifteen fertile eggs, and a pair of rabbits. Pretty soon we had meat of our own. We always let Peggy think that the fryers we ate came from the Schultzes and I don't think she ever caught on. At first I used to go to the

Schultz farm every day for fresh milk for Peggy, but I got a chance, midsummer, to get a fresh two-year-old cow on tick at a reasonable price. Peggy named her Mabel and was much irked that she couldn't get at her to pet her.

We were on the move all the time. I still hadn't managed to take my merit badge tests and I hadn't done much better about getting in to Scout meetings. There was just too much to do. Building a pond, for example—Laguna Serenidad was being infected with plankton and algae but there weren't fish in it yet and it would be a long time, even after the fish were stocked, before fishing would be allowed. So we did fish-pond gardening, Chinese style, after I got the pond built.

And there were always crops to work on. My cover grass had taken hold all right and shortly after we moved in the soil seemed ready to take angle worms. Dad was about to send a sample into town for analysis when Papa Schultz stopped by. Hearing what we were about he took up a handful of the worked soil, crumbled it, smelled it, tasted it, and told me to go ahead and plant my worms. I did and they did all right; we encountered them from time to time in working the fields thereafter.

You could see the stripes on the fields which had been planted with pay dirt by the way the grass came up. You could see that the infection was spreading, too, but not much. I had a lot of hard work ahead before the stripes would meet and blend together and then we could think about renting a cud-chewer and finishing off the other acre and a half, using our own field loam and our own compost heap to infect the new soil. After that we could see about crushing some more acres, but that was a long way away.

We put in carrots and lettuce and beets and cabbage and brussels sprouts and potatoes and broccoli. We planted corn between the rows. I would like to have put in an acre of wheat but it didn't make sense when we had so little land. There was one special little patch close to the house where we put in tomatoes and Hubbard squash and some peas and beans. Those were "bee" plants and Molly would come out and pollenate them by hand, a very tedious business. We hoped to have a hive of bees some day and the entomologists on the bionomics staff were practically busting their hearts trying to breed a strain of bees which would prosper out doors. You see, among other things, while our gravity was only a third Earth-normal, our air pressure was only a little better than a fifth Earth-normal and the bees resented it; it made flying hard work for them.

Or maybe bees are just naturally conservative.

I guess I was happy, or too tired and too busy to be unhappy, right up to the following winter.

At first winter seemed like a good rest. Aside from getting the ice crop in and taking care of the cow and the rabbits and the chickens there wasn't too much to do. I was tired out and cranky and didn't know it; Molly, I think, was just quietly, patiently exhausted. She wasn't used to farm life and she wasn't handy at it, the way Mama Schultz was.

Besides that, she wanted inside plumbing and it just wasn't in the cards for her to have it any time soon. I carried water for her, of course, usually having to crack ice in the stream to get it, but that didn't cover everything, not with snow on the ground. Not that she complained.

Dad didn't complain, either, but there were deep lines forming from his nose down to his mouth which his beard didn't cover entirely. But it was mostly Peggy.

When we first moved her out to the farm she perked up a lot. We gradually reduced the pressure in her room and she kept insisting that she was fine and teasing for a chance to go out without the bubble stretcher. We even tried it once, on Dr. Archibald's advice, and she didn't have a nose bleed but she was willing to get back in after about ten minutes.

The fact was she wasn't adjusting. It wasn't just the pressure; something else was wrong. She didn't *belong* here and she wouldn't *grow* here. Have you ever had a plant that refused to be happy where you planted it? It was like that.

She belonged back on Earth.

I suppose we weren't bad off, but there is a whale of a difference between being a rich farmer, like Papa Schultz, with heaps of cow manure in your barn yard and hams hanging in your cold cellar and every modern convenience you could want, even running water in your house, and being poor framers, like us, scratching for a toe hold in new soil and in debt to the Commission. It told on us and that winter we had time to brood about it.

We were all gathered in Peggy's room after lunch one Thursday. Dark phase had just started and Dad was due to go back into town; we always gave him a send off. Molly was darning and Peg and George were playing cribbage. I got out my squeeze box and started knocking out some tunes. I guess we all felt cheerful enough for a while. I don't know how I happened to drift into it, but after a bit I found I was playing *The Green Hills of Earth*. I hadn't played it in a long time.

I brayed through that fortissimo part about "*Out ride the sons of Terra; Far drives the thundering jet——*" and was thinking to myself that jets didn't thunder any more. I was still thinking about it when I went on into the last chorus, the one you play very softly: "*We pray for one last landing on the globe that gave us birth——*"

I looked up and there were tears running down Molly's cheeks.

I could have kicked myself. I put my accordion down with a squawk, not even finishing, and got up. Dad said, "What's the matter, Bill?"

I muttered something about having to go take a look at Mabel.

I went out into the living room and put on my heavy clothes and actually did go outside, though I didn't go near the barn. It had been snowing and it was already almost pitch dark, though the Sun hadn't been down more than a couple of hours. The snow had stopped but there were clouds over head and you couldn't see Jupiter.

The clouds had broken due west and let the sunset glow come through a bit. After my eyes adjusted, by that tiny amount of light I could see around me—the mountains, snow to their bases, disappearing in the clouds, the lake, just a sheet of snow-covered ice, and the boulders beyond our fields, making weird shapes in the snow. It was a scene to match the way I felt; it looked like the place where you might be sent for having lived a long and sinful life.

I tried to figure out what I was doing in such a place.

The clouds in the west shifted a little and I saw a single bright green star, low down toward the horizon, just above where the Sun had set.

It was Earth.

I don't know how long I stood there. Presently somebody put a hand on my shoulder and I jumped. It was Dad, all bundled up for a nine-mile tramp through the dark and the snow.

"What's the matter, Son?" he said.

I started to speak, but I was all choked up and couldn't. Finally I managed to say, "Dad, why did we come here?"

"Mmmm . . . you wanted to come. Remember?"

"I know," I admitted.

"Still, the real reason, the basic reason, for coming here was to keep your grandchildren from starving. Earth is overcrowded, Bill."

I looked back at Earth again. Finally I said, "Dad, I've made a discovery. There's more to life than three square meals a day. Sure, we can make crops here—this land would grow hair on a billiard ball. But I don't think you had better plan on any grandchildren here; it would be no favor to them. I know when I've made a mistake."

"You're wrong, Bill. *Your* kids will like this place, just the way Eskimos like where they live."

"I doubt it like the mischief."

"Remember, the ancestors of Eskimos weren't Eskimos; they were immigrants, too. If you send your kids back to Earth, for school, say, they'll be homesick for Ganymede. They'll *hate* Earth. They'll weigh too much, they won't like the air, they won't like the climate, they won't like the people."

"Hmm—look, George, do you like it here? Are you glad we came?"

Dad was silent for a long time. At last he said, "I'm worried about Peggy, Bill."

"Yeah, I know. But how about yourself—and Molly?"

"I'm not worried about Molly. Women have their ups and downs. You'll learn to expect that." He shook himself and said, "I'm late. You go on inside and have Molly fix you a cup of tea. Then take a look at the rabbits. I think the doe is about to drop again; we don't want to lose the young 'uns." He hunched his shoulders and set off down toward the road. I watched him out of sight and then went back inside.

16. Line Up

Then suddenly it was spring and everything was all right.

Even winter seemed like a good idea when it was gone. We had to have winter; the freezing and thawing was necessary to develop the ground, not to mention the fact that many crops won't come to fruit without cold weather. Anyway, anybody can live through four weeks of bad weather.

Dad laid off his job when spring came and we pitched in together and got our fields planted. I rented a power barrow and worked across my strips to spread the living soil. Then there was the back-breaking job of preparing the gully for the apple trees. I had started the seeds soon after Papa Schultz had given them to me, forcing them indoors, first at the Schultz's, then at our place. Six of them had germinated and now they were nearly two feet tall.

I wanted to try them outdoors. Maybe I would have to take them in again next winter, but it was worth a try.

Dad was interested in the venture, too, not just for fruit trees, but for lumber. Wood seems like an obsolete material, but try getting along without it.

I think George had visions of the Big Rock Candy

Mountains covered with tall straight pines . . . someday, someday.

So we went deep and built it to drain and built it wide and used a lot of our winter compost and some of our precious topsoil. There was room enough for twenty trees when we got through, where we planted our six little babies. Papa Schultz came over and pronounced a benediction over them.

Then he went inside to say hello to Peggy, almost filling her little room. George used to say that when Papa inhaled the pressure in the room dropped.

A bit later Papa and Dad were talking in the living room; Dad stopped me as I was passing through. "Bill," he asked, "how would you like to have a window about here?" He indicated a blank wall.

I stared. "Huh? How would we keep the place warm?"

"I mean a real window, with glass."

"Oh." I thought about it. I had never lived in a place with windows in my life; we had always been apartment dwellers. I had *seen* windows, of course, in country houses back Earthside, but there wasn't a window on Ganymede and it hadn't occurred to me that there ever would be.

"Papa Schultz plans to put one in his house. I thought it might be nice to sit inside and look out over the lake, light phase evenings," Dad went on.

"To make a home you need windows and fireplaces," Papa said placidly. "Now that we glass make, I mean to have a view."

Dad nodded. "For three hundred years the race had glazed windows. Then they shut themselves up in little air-conditioned boxes and stared at silly television pictures instead. One might as well be on Luna."

It was a startling idea, but it seemed like a good one. I knew they were making glass in town. George says that glassmaking is one of the oldest manufacturing arts, if not the oldest, and certainly one of the simplest. But I had thought about it for bottles and dishes, not for window glass. They already had glass buckets on sale at the 'Change, for about a tenth the cost of the imported article.

A view window—it was a nice idea. We could put one on the south and see the lake and another on the north and see the mountains. Why, I could even put in a skylight and lie on my bunk and see old Jupiter.

Stow it, William, I said to myself; you'll be building a whole house out of glass next. After Papa Schultz left I spoke to George about it. "Look," I said, "about this view window idea. It's a good notion, especially for Peggy's room, but the question is: can we afford it?"

"I think we can," he answered.

"I mean can we afford it without your going back to work in town? You've been working yourself to death —and there's no need to. The farm can support us now."

He nodded. "I had been meaning to speak about that. I've about decided to give up the town work, Bill—except for a class I'll teach on Saturdays."

"Do you have to do that?"

"Happens that I like to teach engineering, Bill. And don't worry about the price of the glass; we'll get it free—a spot of cumshaw coming to your old man for designing the glass works. 'The kine who tread the grain,' " he quoted. "Now you and I had better get busy; there is a rain scheduled for fifteen o'clock."

It was maybe three weeks later that the moons lined up. This is an event that almost never happens, Ganymede, Callisto, Io, and Europa, all perfectly lined up and all on the same side of Jupiter. They come close to lining up every seven hundred and two days, but they don't quite make it ordinarily. You see, their periods are all different, from less than two days for Io to more than two weeks for Callisto and the fractions don't work out evenly. Besides that they have different eccentricities to their orbits and their orbits aren't exactly in the same plane.

As you can see, a real line up hardly ever happens.

Besides that, *this* line up was a line up with the Sun, too; it would occur at Jupiter full phase. Mr. Hooker, the chief meteorologist, announced that it had been calculated that such a perfect line up would not occur again for more than two hundred thousand years. You can bet we were all waiting to see it. The Project Jove scientists were excited about it, too, and special arrangements had been made to observe it.

Having it occur at Jupiter full phase meant not only that a sixth heavenly body—the Sun—would be in the line up, but that we would be able to see it. The shadows of Ganymede and Callisto would be centered on Jupiter just as Io and Europa reached mid transit.

Full phase is at six o'clock Saturday morning; we all got up about four-thirty and were outside by five. George and I carried Peggy out in her bubble stretcher. We were just in time.

It was a fine, clear summer night, light as could be, with old Jupiter blazing overhead like a balloon on fire. Io had just barely kissed the eastern edge of Jupiter—"first contact" they call it. Europa was already a bit inside the eastern edge and I had to look sharp to see it. When a moon is not in full phase it is no trouble to pick it out while it's making its transit, but at full phase it tends to blend into the background. However, both Io and Europa are just a hair brighter than Jupiter. Besides that, they break up the pattern of Jupiter's bands and that lets you see them, too.

Well inside, but still in the eastern half—say about half way to Jupiter's center point—were the shadows of Ganymede and Callisto. I could not have told them apart, if I hadn't known that the one further east had to be Ganymede's. They were just little round black dots; three thousand miles or so isn't anything when it's plastered against Jupiter's eighty-nine thousand mile width.

Io looked a bit bigger than the shadows; Europa

looked more than half again as big, about the way the Moon looks from Earth.

We felt a slight quake but it wasn't even enough to make us nervous; we were used to quakes. Besides that, about then Io "kissed" Europa. From then on, throughout the rest of the show, Io gradually slid underneath, or behind, Europa.

They crawled across the face of Jupiter; the moons fairly fast, the shadows in a slow creep. When we had been outside a little less than half an hour the two shadows kissed and started to merge. Io had slid halfway under Europa and looked like a big tumor on its side. They were almost halfway to center and the shadows were even closer.

Just before six o'clock Europa—you could no longer see Io; Europa covered it—as I was saying, Europa kissed the shadow, which by now was round, just one shadow.

Four or five minutes later the shadow had crawled up on top of Europa; they were all lined up—and I knew I was seeing the most extraordinary sight I would ever see in my life, Sun, Jupiter, and the four biggest moons all perfectly lined up.

I let out a deep breath: I don't know how long I had been holding it. "Gee whiz!" was all I could think of to say.

"I agree in general with your sentiments, Bill," Dad answered. "Molly, hadn't we better get Peggy inside? I'm afraid she is getting cold."

"Yes," agreed Molly. "I know I am, for one."

"I'm going down to the lake now," I said. The biggest tide of record was expected, of course. While the lake was too small to show much tide, I had made a mark the day before and I hoped to be able to measure it.

"Don't get lost in the dark," Dad called out. I didn't answer him. A silly remark doesn't require an answer.

I had gotten past the road and maybe a quarter of a mile beyond when it hit.

It knocked me flat on my face, the heaviest shake I had ever felt in my life. I've felt heavy quakes in California; they weren't a patch on this one. I lay face down for a long moment, digging into the rock with my finger nails and trying to get it to *hold still*.

The seasick roll kept up and kept up and kept up, and with it the noise—a deep bass rumble, deeper than thunder and more terrifying.

A rock rolled up against me and nipped my side. I got to my feet and managed to stay there. The ground was still swaying and the rumble kept on. I headed for the house, running—like dancing over shifting ice. I fell down twice and got up again.

The front end of the house was all caved in. The roof slanted down at a crazy angle. "George!" I yelled. "Molly! Where are you?"

George heard me and straightened up. He was on the other side of the house and now I saw him over the collapsed roof. He didn't say anything. I rushed around to where he stood. "Are you all right?" I demanded.

"Help me get Molly out——" he gasped.

I found out later that George had gone inside with Molly and Peggy, had helped get Peg out of the stretcher and back into her room, and then had gone outside, leaving Molly to get breakfast. The quake had hit while he was returning from the barn. But we didn't have time then to talk it over; we dug—moving slabs with our bare hands that had taken four Scouts, working together, to lay. George kept crying, "Molly! Molly! Where are you?"

She was lying on the floor beside the stone work bench that was penned in by the roof. We heaved it off her; George scrambled over the rubble and reached her. "Molly! Molly darling!"

She opened her eyes. "George!"

"Are you all right?"

"What happened?"

"Quake. Are you all right? Are you hurt?"

She sat up, made a face as if something hurt her,

and said, "I think I—— George! Where's Peggy? *Get Peggy!*"

Peggy's room was still upright; the reinforcements had held while the rest of the house had gone down around it. George insisted on moving Molly out into the open first, then we tackled the slabs that kept us from getting at the air lock to Peggy's room.

The outer door of the air lock was burst out of its gaskets and stood open, the wrong way. It was black inside the lock; Jupiter light didn't reach inside. I couldn't see what I was doing but when I pushed on the inner door it wouldn't give. "Can't budge it," I told Dad. "Get a light."

"Probably still held by air pressure. Call out to Peggy to get in the stretcher and we'll bleed it."

"I need a light," I repeated.

"I haven't got a light."

"Didn't you have one with you?" *I* had had one; we always carried torches, outdoors in dark phase, but I had dropped mine when the quake hit. I didn't know where it was.

Dad thought about it, then climbed over the slabs. He was back in a moment. "I found it between here and the barn. I must have dropped it." He shined it on the inner door and we looked over the situation.

"It looks bad," Dad said softly. "Explosive decompression." There was a gap you could poke your fingers through between the top of the door and the frame; the door wasn't pressure held, it was jammed.

Dad called out, "Peggy! Oh, Peggy, darling—can you hear me?"

No answer. "Take the light, Bill—and stand aside." He reared back and then hit the door hard with his shoulder. It gave a bit but didn't open. He hit it again and it flew open, spilling him on his hands and knees. He scrambled up as I shined the light in past him.

Peggy lay half in and half out of bed, as if she had

been trying to get up when she passed out. Her head hung down and a trickle of blood was dripping from her mouth on to the floor.

Molly had come in right behind us; she and Dad got Peggy into the stretcher and Dad brought the pressure up. She was alive; she gasped and choked and sprayed blood over us while we were trying to help her. Then she cried. She seemed to quiet down and go to sleep —or maybe fainted again—after we got her into the bubble.

Molly was crying but not making any fuss about it. Dad straightened up, wiped his face and said, "Grab on, Bill. We've got to get her into town."

I said, "Yes," and picked up one end. With Molly holding the light and us carrying, we picked our way over the heap of rock that used to be our house and got out into the open. We put the stretcher down for a moment and I looked around.

I glanced up at Jupiter; the shadows were still on his face and Io and Europa had not yet reached the western edge. The whole thing had taken less than an hour. But that wasn't what held my attention; the sky looked funny.

The stars were too bright and there were too many of them. "George," I said, "what's happened to the sky?"

"No time now——" he started to say. Then he stopped and said very slowly, "Great Scott!"

"What?" asked Molly. "What's the matter?"

"Back to the house, all of you! We've got to dig out all the clothes we can get at. And blankets!"

"What? Why?"

"The heat trap! The heat trap is gone—the quake must have gotten the power house."

So we dug again, until we found what we had to have. It didn't take long; we knew where things had to be. It was just a case of getting the rocks off. The blankets were for the stretcher; Dad wrapped them around like a cocoon and tied them in place. "Okay, Bill," he said. "Quick march, now!"

It was then that I heard Mabel bawl. I stopped and looked at Dad. He stopped too, with an agony of indecision on his face. "Oh, damn!" he said, the first time I had ever heard him really swear. "We can't just leave her to freeze; she's a member of the family. Come, Bill."

We put the stretcher down again and ran to the barn. It was a junk heap but we could tell by Mabel's complaints where she was. We dragged the roof off her and she got to her feet. She didn't seem to be hurt but I guess she had been knocked silly. She looked at us indignantly.

We had a time of it getting her over the slabs, with Dad pulling and me pushing. Dad handed the halter to Molly. "How about the chickens?" I asked, "And the rabbits?" Some of them had been crushed; the rest were loose around the place. I felt one—a rabbit —scurry between my feet.

"No time!" snapped Dad. "We can't take them; all we could do for them would be to cut their throats. Come!"

We headed for the road.

Molly led the way, leading and dragging Mabel and carrying the light. We needed the light. The night, too bright and too clear a few minutes before, was now suddenly overcast. Shortly we couldn't see Jupiter at all, and then you couldn't count your fingers in front of your face.

The road was wet underfoot, not rain, but sudden dew; it was getting steadily colder.

Then it did rain, steadily and coldly. Presently it changed to wet snow. Molly dropped back. "George," she wanted to know, "have we come as far as the turn off to the Schultz's?"

"That's no good," he answered. "We've got to get the baby into the hospital."

"That isn't what I meant. Oughtn't I to warn them?"

"They'll be all right. Their house is sound."

"But the cold?"

"Oh." He saw what she meant and so did I, when I thought about it. With the heat trap gone and the power house gone, every house in the colony was going to be like an ice box. What good is a power receiver on your roof with no power to receive? It was going to get colder and colder and colder . . . .

And then it would get colder again. And colder. . . .

"Keep moving," Dad said suddenly. "We'll figure it out when we get there."

But we didn't figure it out, because we never found the turn off. The snow was driving into our faces by then and we must have walked on past it. It was a dry snow now, little sharp needles that burned when they hit.

Without saying anything about it, I had started counting paces when we left the walls of lava that marked the place where the new road led to our place and out to the new farms beyond. As near as I could make it we had come about five miles when Molly stopped. "What's the matter?" yelled Dad.

"Dear," she said, "I can't find the road. I think I've lost it."

I kicked the snow away underfoot. It was made ground, all right—soft. Dad took the torch and looked at his watch. "We must have come about six miles," he announced.

"Five," I corrected him. "Or five and a half at the outside," I told him I had been counting.

He considered it. "We've come just about to that stretch where the road is flush with the field," he said. "It can't be more than a half mile or a mile to the cut through Kneiper's Ridge. After that we can't lose it. Bill, take the light and cast off to the right for a hundred paces, then back to the left. If that doesn't do it, we'll go further. And for heaven's sakes retrace your steps—it's the only way you'll find us in this storm."

I took the light and set out. To the right was no good, though I went a hundred and fifty paces instead of a hundred, I got back to them, and reported, and started out again. Dad just grunted; he was busy with something about the stretcher.

On the twenty-third step to the left I found the road —by stepping down about a foot, falling flat on my face, and nearly losing the light. I picked myself up and went back.

"Good!" said Dad. "Slip your neck through this."

"This" was a sort of yoke he had devised by retying the blankets around the stretcher so as to get some free line. With my neck through it I could carry the weight on my shoulders and just steady my end with my hands. Not that it was heavy, but our hands were getting stiff with cold. "Good enough!" I said, "But, look, George—let Molly take your end."

"Nonsense!"

"It isn't nonsense. Molly can do it—can't you, Molly? And you know this road better than we do; you've tramped it enough times in the dark."

"Bill is right, dear," Molly said at once. "Here—take Mabel."

Dad gave in, took the light and the halter. Mabel didn't want to go any further; she wanted to sit down, I guess. Dad kicked her in the rear and jerked on her neck. Her feelings were hurt; she wasn't used to that sort of treatment—particularly not from Dad. But there was no time to humor her; it was getting colder.

We went on. I don't know how Dad kept to the road but he did. We had been at it another hour, I suppose, and had left Kneiper's slot well behind, when Molly stumbled, then her knees just seemed to cave in and she knelt down in the snow.

I stopped and sat down, too; I needed the rest. I just wanted to stay there and let it snow.

Dad came back and put his arms around her and comforted her and told her to lead Mabel now; she couldn't get lost on this stretch. She insisted that she

could still carry. Dad ignored her, just lifted the yoke
business off her shoulders. Then he came back and
peeled a bit of blanket off the bubble and shined the
torch inside. He put it back into place. Molly said,
"How is she?"

Dad said, "She's still breathing. She opened her eyes
when the light hit them. Let's go." He got the yoke on
and Molly took the light and the halter.

Molly couldn't have seen what I saw; the plastic of
the bubble was frosted over on the inside. Dad hadn't
seen Peggy breathe; he hadn't seen anything.

I thought about it for a long while and wondered
how you would classify that sort of a lie. Dad wasn't
a liar, that was certain—and yet it seemed to me that
such a lie, right then, was better than the truth. It was
complicated.

Pretty soon I forgot it; I was too busy putting one
foot in front of the other and counting the steps. I
couldn't feel my feet any longer.

Dad stopped and I bumped into the end of the
stretcher. "Listen!" he said.

I listened and heard a dull rumble. "Quake?"

"No. Keep quiet." Then he added, "It's down the
road. Off the road, everybody! Off to the right."

The rumble got louder and presently I made out a
light through the snow, back the way we had come.
Dad saw it, too, and stepped out on the road and
started waving our torch.

The rumble stopped almost on top of him; it was a
rock crusher and it was loaded down with people,
people clinging to it all over and even riding the spade.
The driver yelled, "Climb on! And hurry!"

Then he saw the cow and added, "No live stock."

"We've got a stretcher with my little girl in it," Dad
shouted back to him. "We need help."

There was a short commotion, while the driver or-
dered a couple of men down to help us. In the mix
up Dad disappeared. One moment Molly was hólding
Mabel's halter, then Dad was gone and so was the cow.

We got the stretcher up onto the spade and some of the men braced it with their backs. I was wondering what to do about Dad and thinking maybe I ought to jump off and look for him, when he appeared out of the darkness and scrambled up beside me. "Where's Molly?" he asked.

"Up on top. But where is Mabel? What did you do with her?"

Mabel is all right." He folded his knife and put it in his pocket. I didn't ask any more questions.

17. Disaster

We passed several more people after that, but the driver wouldn't stop. We were fairly close into town and he insisted that they could make it on their own. His emergency power pack was running low, he said; he had come all the way from the bend in the lake, ten miles beyond our place.

Besides, I don't know where he would have put them. We were about three deep and Dad had to keep warning people not to lean on the bubble of the stretcher.

Then the power pack did quit and the driver shouted, "Everybody off! Get on in on your own." But by now we were actually in town, the outskirts, and it would have been no trouble if it hadn't been blowing a blizzard. The driver insisted on helping Dad with the stretcher. He was a good Joe and turned out to be—when I saw him in the light—the same man who had crushed our acreage.

At long, long last we were inside the hospital and Peggy was turned over to the hospital people and put in a pressurized room. More than that, she was alive. In bad shape, but alive.

Molly stayed with her. I would like to have stayed, too—it was fairly warm in the hospital; it had its own emergency power pack. But they wouldn't let me.

Dad told Molly that he was reporting to the chief engineer for duty. I was told to go to the Immigration Receiving Station. I did so and it was just like the day we landed, only worse—and colder. I found myself right back in the very room which was the first I had ever been in on Ganymede.

The place was packed and getting more packed every minute as more refugees kept pouring in from the surrounding country. It was cold, though not so bitterly cold as outside. The lights were off, of course; light and heat all came from the power plant for everything. Hand lights had been set up here and there and you could sort of grope your way around. There were the usual complaints, too, though maybe not as bad as you hear from immigrants. I paid no attention to any of them; I was happy in a dead beat sort of way just to be inside and fairly warm and feel the blood start to go back into my feet.

We stayed there for thirty-seven hours. It was twenty-four hours before we got anything to eat.

Here was the way it went: the metal buildings, such as the Receiving Station, stood up. Very few of the stone buildings had, which we knew by then from the reports of all of us. The Power Station was out, and with it, the heat trap. They wouldn't tell us anything about it except to say that it was being fixed.

In the mean time we were packed in tight as they could put us, keeping the place warm mainly by the heat from our bodies, sheep style. There were, they say, several power packs being used to heat the place, too, one being turned on every time the temperature in the room dropped below freezing. If so, I never got close to one and I don't think it ever did get *up* to freezing where I was.

I would sit down and grab my knees and fall into a dopey sleep. Then a nightmare would wake me up and I'd get up and pound myself and walk around. After a while I'd sit down on the floor and freeze my fanny again.

I seem to remember encountering Noisy Edwards in the crowd and waving my finger under his nose and telling him I had an appointment to knock his block off. I seem to remember him staring back at me as if he couldn't place me. But I don't know; I may have dreamed it. I thought I ran across Hank, too, and had a long talk with him, but Hank told me afterwards that he never laid eyes on me the whole time.

After a long time—it seemed a week but the records show it was eight o'clock Sunday morning—they passed us out some lukewarm soup. It was wonderful. After that I wanted to leave the building to go to the hospital. I wanted to find Molly and see how Peggy was doing.

They wouldn't let me. It was seventy below outside and still dropping.

About twenty-two o'clock the lights came on and the worst was over.

We had a decent meal soon after that, sandwiches and soup, and when the Sun came up at midnight they announced that anybody could go outside who cared to risk it. I waited until noon Monday. By then it was up to twenty below and I made a dash for it to the hospital.

Peggy was doing as well as could be expected. Molly had stayed with her and had spent the time in bed with her, huddling up to her to keep her warm. While the hospital had emergency heat, it didn't have the capacity to cope with any such disaster as had struck us; it was darn near as cold as the Receiving Station. But Peggy had come through it, sleeping most of the time. She even perked up enough to smile and say hello.

Molly's left arm was in a sling and splinted. I asked how that happened—and then I felt foolish. It had happened in the quake itself but I hadn't known it and George still didn't know about it; none of the engineers were back.

It didn't seem possible that she could have done what she did, until I recalled that she carried the stretcher only after Dad had rigged the rope yokes. Molly is all right.

They chased me out and I high-tailed it back to the Receiving Station and ran into Sergei almost at once. He hailed me and I went over to him. He had a pencil and a list and a number of the older fellows were gathered around him. "What's up?" I said.

"Just the guy I'm looking for," he said. "I had you down for dead. Disaster party—are you in?"

I was in, all right. The parties were made up of older Scouts, sixteen and up, and the younger men. We were sent out on the town's tractors, one to each road, and we worked in teams of two. I spotted Hank Jones as we were loading and they let us make up a team.

It was grim work. For equipment we had shovels and lists—lists of who lived on which farm. Sometimes a name would have a notation "known to be alive," but more often not. A team would be dropped off with the lists for three or four farms and the tractor would go on, to pick them up on the return trip.

Our job was to settle the doubt about those other names and—theoretically—to rescue anyone still alive.

We didn't find anyone alive.

The lucky ones had been killed in the quake; the unlucky ones had waited too long and didn't make it into town. Some we found on the road; they had tried to make it but had started too late. The worst of all were those whose houses hadn't fallen and had tried to stick it out. Hank and I found one couple just sitting, arms around each other. They were hard as rock.

When we found one, we would try to identify it on the list, then cover it up with snow, several feet deep, so it would keep for a while after it started to thaw.

When we settled with the people at a farm, we rummaged around and found all the livestock we could and carried or dragged their carcasses down to the road, to be toted into town on the tractor and slapped into deep freeze. It seemed a dirty job to do, robbing the dead, but, as Hank pointed out, we would all be getting a little hungry by and by.

Hank bothered me a little; he was merry about the whole thing. I guess it was better to laugh about it, in the long run, and after a while he had me doing it. It was just too big to soak up all at once and you didn't dare let it get you.

But I should have caught on when we came to his own place. "We can skip it," he said, and checked off the list.

"Hadn't we better check for livestock?" I said.

"Nope. We're running short of time. Let's move on to the Millers' place."

"Did they get out?"

"I don't know. I didn't see any of them in town."

The Millers hadn't gotten out; we barely had time to take care of them before the tractor picked us up. It was a week later that I found out that both of Hank's parents had been killed in the quake. He had taken time to drag them out and put them into their ice cellar before he had headed for town.

Like myself, Hank had been outside when it hit, still looking at the line up. The fact that the big shock had occurred right after the line up had kept a lot of people from being killed in their beds—but they say that the line up caused the quake, triggered it, that is, with tidal strains, so I guess it sort of evens up. Of course, the line up didn't actually make the quake; it had been building up to it ever since the beginning of the atmosphere project. Gravity's books have got to balance.

The colony had had thirty-seven thousand people when the quake hit. The census when we finished it showed less than thirteen thousand. Besides that we had lost every crop, all or almost all the livestock. As Hank said, we'd all be a little hungry by and by.

They dumped us back at the Receiving Station and a second group of parties got ready to leave. I looked for a quiet spot to try to get some sleep.

I was just dozing off, it seemed to me, when somebody shook me. It was Dad. "Are you all right, Bill?"

I rubbed my eyes. "I'm okay. Have you seen Molly and Peggy?"

"Just left them. I'm off duty for a few hours. Bill, have you seen anything of the Schultzes?"

I sat up, wide awake. "No. Have you?"

"No."

I told him what I had been doing and he nodded. "Go back to sleep, Bill. I'll see if there has been a report on them."

I didn't go to sleep. He was back after a bit to say that he hadn't been able to find out anything one way or another. "I'm worried, Bill."

"So am I."

"I'm going out and check up."

"Let's go."

Dad shook his head. "No need for us both. You get some sleep." I went along, just the same.

We were lucky. A disaster party was just heading down our road and we hitched a ride. Our own farm and the Schultz's place were among those to be covered on this trip; Dad told the driver that we would check both places and report when we got back to town. That was all right with him.

They dropped us at the turn off and we trudged up toward the Schultz's house. I began to get the horrors as we went. It's one thing to pile snow over comparative strangers; it's another thing entirely to expect to find Mama Schultz or Gretchen with their faces blue and stiff.

I didn't visualize Papa as dead; people like Papa Schultz don't die—they just go on forever. Or it feels like that.

But I still wasn't prepared for what we did find.

We had just come around a little hummock that conceals their house from the road. George stopped and said, "Well, the house is still standing. His quake-proofing held."

I looked at it, then I stared—and then I yelled. "Hey, George! *The Tree is gone!*"

The house was there, but the apple tree—"the most beautiful tree on Ganymede"—was missing. Just gone. I began to run.

We were almost to the house when the door opened. There stood Papa Schultz.

They were all safe, every one of them. What remained of the tree was ashes in the fireplace. Papa had cut it down as soon as the power went off and the temperature started to drop—and then had fed it, little by little, into the flames.

Papa, telling us about it, gestured at the blackened firebox. "Johann's folly, they called it. I guess they will not think old Appleseed Johnny quite so foolish now, eh?" He roared and slapped Dad on the shoulders.

"But your tree," I said stupidly.

"I will plant another, many others." He stopped and was suddenly serious. "But your trees, William, your brave little baby trees—they are dead, not?"

I said I hadn't seen them yet. He nodded solemnly. "They are dead of the cold. Hugo!"

"Yes, Papa."

"Fetch me an apple." Hugo did so and Papa presented it to me. "You will plant again." I nodded and stuck it in my pocket.

They were glad to hear that we were all right, though Mama clucked over Molly's broken arm. Yo had fought his way over to our place during the first part of the storm, found that we were gone and returned, two frost bitten ears for his efforts. He was in town now to look for us.

But they were all right, every one of them. Even their livestock they had saved—cows, pigs, chickens, people, all huddled together throughout the cold and kept from freezing by the fire from their tree.

The animals were back in the barn, now that power was on again, but the place still showed that they had been there—and smelled of it, too. I think Mama was more upset by the shambles of her immaculate living room than she was by the magnitude of the disaster. I don't think she realized that most of her neighbors were dead. It hadn't hit her yet.

Dad turned down Papa Schultz's offer to come with us to look over our farm. Then Papa said he would see us on the tractor truck, as he intended to go into town and find out what he could do. We had mugs of Mama's strong tea and some corn bread and left.

I was thinking about the Schultzes and how good it was to find them alive, as we trudged over to our place. I told Dad that it was a miracle.

He shook his head. "Not a miracle. They are survivor types."

"What type is a survivor type?" I asked.

He took a long time to answer that one. Finally he said, "Survivors survive. I guess that is the only way to tell the survivor type for certain."

I said, "We're survivor types, too, in that case."

"Could be," he admitted. "At least we've come through this one."

When I had left, the house was down. In the mean time I had seen dozens of houses down, yet it was a shock to me when we topped the rise and I saw that it really was down. I suppose I expected that after a while I would wake up safe and warm in bed and everything would be all right.

The fields were there, that was all that you could say for it. I scraped the snow off a stretch I knew was beginning to crop. The plants were dead of course and the ground was hard. I was fairly sure that even

the earth worms were dead; they had had nothing
to warn them to burrow below the frost line.

My little saplings were dead, of course.

We found two of the rabbits, huddled together and
stiff, under a drift against what was left of the barn.
We didn't find any of the chickens except one, the
first old hen we ever had. She had been setting and
her nest wasn't crushed and had been covered by a
piece of the fallen roof of the barn. She was still
on it, hadn't moved and the eggs under her were
frozen. I think that was what got me.

I was just a chap who used to have a farm.

Dad had been poking around the house. He came
back to the barn and spoke to me. "Well, Bill?"

I stood up. "George, I've had it."

"Then let's go back to town. The truck will be
along shortly."

"I mean I've really had it!"

"Yes, I know."

I took a look in Peggy's room first, but Dad's salvage had been thorough. My accordion was in there,
however, with snow from the broken door drifted over
the case. I brushed it off and picked it up. "Leave
it," Dad said. "It's safe here and you've no place to
put it."

"I don't expect to be back," I said.

"Very well."

We made a bundle of what Dad had gotten together, added the accordion, the two rabbits and the
hen, and carried it all down to the road. The tractor
showed up presently, we got aboard and Dad chucked
the rabbits and chicken on the pile of such that they
had salvaged. Papa Schultz was waiting at his turnoff.

Dad and I tried to spot Mabel by the road on the
trip back, but we didn't find her. Probably she had
been picked up by an earlier trip, seeing that she was
close to town. I was just as well pleased. All right,

she had to be salvaged—but I didn't want the job. I'm not a cannibal.

I managed to get some sleep and a bite to eat and was sent out on another disaster party. The colony began to settle down into some sort of routine. Those whose houses had stood up moved back into them and the rest of us were taken care of in the Receiving Station, much as we had been when our party landed. Food was short, of course, and Ganymede had rationing for the first time since the first colonials really got started.

Not that we were going to starve. In the first place there weren't too many of us to feed and there had been quite a lot of food on hand. The real pinch would come later. It was decided to set winter back by three months, that is, start all over again with spring—which messed up the calendar from then on. But it would give us a new crop as quickly as possible to make up for the one that we had lost.

Dad stayed on duty with the engineer's office. Plans called for setting up two more power plants, spaced around the equator, and each of them capable of holding the heat trap alone. The disaster wasn't going to be allowed to happen again. Of course the installations would have to come from Earth, but we had been lucky on one score; Mars was in a position to relay for us. The report had gone into Earth at once and, instead of another load of immigrants, we were to get what we needed on the next trip.

Not that I cared. I had stayed in town, too, although the Schultzes had invited me to stay with them. I was earning my keep helping to rebuild and quakeproof the houses of the survivors. It had been agreed that we would all go back, George, Molly, Peggy, and me, on the first trip, if we could get space. It had been unanimous except that Peggy hadn't been consulted; it just had to be.

We weren't the only ones who were going back. The Colonial Commission had put up a squawk of course, but under the circumstances they had to give in. After it had been made official and the lists were opened Dad and I went over to the Commission agent's office to put in our applications. We were about the last to apply; Dad had been out of town on duty and I had waited until he got back.

The office was closed with a "Back in a half hour" sign stuck on the door. We waited. There were bulletin boards outside the office; on them were posted the names of those who had applied for repatriation. I started reading them to kill time and so did Dad.

I found Saunders' name there and pointed it out to George. He grunted and said, "No loss." Noisy Edwards' name was there, too; maybe I *had* seen him in the Receiving Station, although I hadn't seen him since. It occurred to me that I could probably corner him in the ship and pay him back his lumps, but I wasn't really interested in the project. I read on down.

I expected to find Hank Jones' name there, but I couldn't find it. I started reading the list carefully, paying attention to every name I recognized. I began to see a pattern.

Presently the agent got back and opened the door. Dad touched my arm. "Come on, Bill."

I said, "Wait a minute, George. You read all the names?"

"Yes, I did."

"I've been thinking. You know, George, I don't *like* being classed with these lugs."

He chewed his lip. "I know exactly what you mean."

I took the plunge. "You can do as you like, George, but I'm not going home, if I ever do, until I've licked this joint."

Dad looked as unhappy as he could look. He was silent for a long time, then he said, "I've got to take

Peggy back, Bill. She won't go unless Molly and I go along. And she's got to go."

"Yes, I know."

"You understand how it is, Bill?"

"Yes, Dad, I understand." He went on in to make out his application, whistling a little tune he used to whistle just after Anne died. I don't think he knew he was whistling it.

I waited for him and after a bit we went away together.

I moved back out to the farm the next day. Not to the Schultzes—to the farm. I slept in Peggy's room and got busy fixing the place up and getting ready to plant my emergency allowance of seed.

Then, about two weeks before they were to leave in the *Covered Wagon*, Peggy died, and there wasn't any reason for any of us to go back to Earth.

Yo Schultz had been in town and Dad sent word back by him. Yo came over and woke me up and told me about it. I thanked him.

He wanted to know if I wanted to come back to the house with him. I said, no, thanks, that I would rather be alone. He made me promise to come over the next day and went away.

I lay back down on Peggy's bed.

She was dead and there was nothing more I could do about it. She was dead and it was all my fault . . . if I hadn't encouraged her, they would have been able to get her to go back before it was too late. She would be back Earthside, going to school and growing up healthy and happy—right back in California, not here in this damned place where she couldn't live, where human beings were never *meant* to live.

I bit the pillow and blubbered. I said, "Oh, Anne, Anne! Take care of her, Anne—She's so little; she won't know what to do."

And then I stopped bawling and listened, half way expecting Anne to answer me and tell me she would.

But I couldn't hear anything, not at first . . . and what I did hear was only, "Stand tall, Billy," . . . very faint and far away, "Stand tall, son."

After a while I got up and washed my face and started hoofing it back into town.

18. Pioneer Party

We all lived in Peggy's room until Dad and I had the seeds in, then we built on to it, quake proof this time and with a big view window facing the lake and another facing the mountains. We knocked a window in Peggy's room, too; it made it seem like a different place.

We built on still another room presently, as it seemed as if we might be needing it. All the rooms had windows and the living room had a fireplace.

Dad and I were terribly busy the second season after the quake. Enough seed could be had by then and we farmed the empty farm across the road from us. Then some newcomers, the Ellises, moved in and paid us for the crop. It was just what they call a "book transaction," but it reduced our debt with the Commission.

Two G-years after the line up you would never have known that anything had happened. There wasn't a wrecked building in the community, there were better than forty-five thousand people, and the town was booming. New people were coming in so fast that you could even sell some produce to the Commission in lieu of land.

We weren't doing so badly, ourselves. We had a hive

of bees. We had Mabel II, and Margie and Mamie, and I was sending the spare milk into town by the city transport truck that passed down our road once a day. I had broken Marge and Mamie to the yoke and used them for ploughing as well—we had crushed five more acres—and we were even talking about getting a horse.

Some people had horses already, the Schultzes for instance. The council had wrangled about it before okaying the "invasion," with conservatives holding out for tractors. But we weren't equipped to manufacture tractors yet and the policy was to make the planet self-sufficient—the hay burners won out. Horses can manufacture more horses and that is one trick that tractors have never learned.

Furthermore, though I would have turned my nose up at the idea when I was a ground hog back in Diego Borough, horse steak is very tasty.

It turned out we did need the extra room. Twins—both boys. New babies don't look as if they were worth keeping, but they get over it—slowly. I bought a crib as a present for them, made right here on Ganymede, out of glass fabric stuck together with synthetic resin. It was getting possible to buy quite a number of home products.

I told Molly I would initiate the brats into the Cubs when they were old enough. I was getting in to meetings oftener now, for I had a patrol again—the Daniel Boone patrol, mostly new kids. I still hadn't taken my own tests but you can't do everything at once. Once I was scheduled to take them and a litter of pigs picked that day to arrive. But I planned to take them; I wanted to be an Eagle Scout again, even if I was getting a little old to worry about badges in themselves.

It may sound as if the survivors didn't give a hoot about those who had died in the disaster. But that isn't the truth. It was just that you work from day to day and that keeps your mind busy. In any case, we

weren't the first colony to be two-thirds wiped out—
and we wouldn't be the last. You can grieve only so
much; after that it's self pity. So George says.

George still wanted me to go back to Earth to finish my education and I had been toying with the idea
myself. I was beginning to realize that there were a
few things I hadn't learned. The idea was attractive;
it would not be like going back right after the quake,
tail between my legs. I'd be a property owner, paying my own way. The fare was considerable—five
acres—and would about clean me out, my half, and
put a load on George and Molly. But they were both
for it.

Besides, Dad owned blocked assets back Earthside
which would pay my way through school. They were
no use to him otherwise; the only thing the Commission will accept as pay for imports is proved land.
There was even a possibility, if the council won a suit
pending back Earthside, that his blocked assets could
be used for my fare as well and not cost us a square
foot of improved soil. All in all, it was nothing to turn
down idly.

We were talking about me leaving on the *New Ark*
when another matter came up—the planetary survey.

Ganymede had to have settlements other than Leda;
that was evident even when we landed. The Commission planned to set up two more ports-of-entry near
the two new power stations and let the place grow
from three centers. The present colonists were to build
the new towns—receiving stations, hydroponics sheds,
infirmaries, and so forth—and be paid for it in imports. Immigration would be stepped up accordingly,
something that the Commission was very anxious to
do, now that they had the ships to dump them in
on us in quantity.

The old *Jitterbug* was about to take pioneer parties
out to select sites and make plans—and both Hank and
Sergei were going.

I wanted to go so bad I could taste it. In the whole time I had been here I had never gotten fifty miles from Leda. Suppose somebody asked me what it was like on Ganymede when I got back on Earth? Truthfully, I wouldn't be able to tell them; I hadn't been any place.

I had had a chance, once, to make a trip to Barnard's Moon, as a temporary employee of Project Jove —and that hadn't worked out either. The twins. I stayed back and took care of the farm.

I talked it over with Dad.

"I hate to see you delay it any longer," he said seriously. I pointed out that it would be only two months.

"Hmmm—" he said. "Have you taken your merit badge tests yet?"

He knew I hadn't; I changed the subject by pointing out that Sergei and Hank were going.

"But they are both older than you are," he answered.

"Not by very much!"

"But I think they are each over the age limit they were looking for—and you are just under."

"Look, George," I protested, "rules were made to be broken. I've heard you say that. There must be some spot I can fill—cook, maybe."

And that's just the job I got—cook.

I always have been a pretty fair cook—not in Mama Schultz's class, but good. The party had nothing to complain about on that score.

Captain Hattie put us down at a selected spot nine degrees north of the equator and longitude 113 west —that is to say, just out of sight of Jupiter on the far side and about thirty-one hundred miles from Leda. Mr. Hooker says that the average temperature of Ganymede will rise about nine degrees over the next century as more and more of the ancient ice melts—at which time Leda will be semi-tropical and the planet will be habitable half way to the poles. In the mean time colonies would be planted only at or near the equator.

I was sorry we had Captain Hattie as pilot; she is such an insufferable old scold. She thinks rocket pilots are a special race apart—supermen. At least she acts like it. Recently the Commission had forced her to take a relief pilot; there was just too much for one pilot to do. They had tried to force a check pilot on her, too—an indirect way to lead up to retiring her, but she was too tough for them. She threatened to take the *Jitterbug* up and crash it . . . and they didn't dare call her bluff. At that time they were absolutely dependent on the *Jitterbug*.

Originally the *Jitterbug's* only purpose was for supply and passengers between Leda and the Project Jove station on Barnard's Moon—but that was back in the days when ships from Earth actually landed at Leda. Then the *Mayflower* came along and the *Jitterbug* was pressed into service as a shuttle. There was talk of another shuttle rocket but we didn't have it yet, which is why Captain Hattie had them where it hurt. The Commission had visions of a loaded ship circling Ganymede, just going round and round and round again, with no way to get down, like a kitten stuck up in a tree.

I'll say this for Hattie; she could handle her ship. I think she had nerve ends out in the skin of it. In clear weather she could even make a glide landing, in spite of our thin air. But I think she preferred to shake up her passengers with a jet landing.

She put us down, the *Jitterbug* took on more water mass, and away it bounced. She had three more parties to land. All in all the *Jitterbug* was servicing eight other pioneer parties. It would be back to pick us up in about three weeks.

The leader of our party was Paul du Maurier, who was the new assistant Scoutmaster of the Auslander troop and the chap who had gotten me taken on as cookie. He was younger than some of those working for him; furthermore, he shaved, which made him stand out like a white leghorn in a hog pen and made him look even younger. That is, he did shave, but he started letting his beard grow on this trip. "Better trim that grass," I advised him.

He said, "Don't you like my beard, Doctor Slop?" —that was a nickname he had awarded me for "Omnibus stew," my own invention. He didn't mean any harm by it.

I said, "Well, it covers your face, which is some help—but you might be mistaken for one of us colonial roughnecks. That wouldn't do for one of you high-toned Commission boys."

He smiled mysteriously and said, "Maybe that's what I want."

I said, "Maybe. But they'll lock you up in a zoo if you wear it back to Earth." He was due to go back for Earthside duty by the same trip I expected to make, via the *Covered Wagon*, two weeks after the end of the survey.

He smiled again and said, "Ah, yes, so they would," and changed the subject. Paul was one of the most thoroughly good guys I have ever met and smart as a whip as well. He was a graduate of South Africa University with P. G. on top of that at the System Institute on Venus—an ecologist, specializing in planetary engineering.

He handled that gang of rugged individualists without raising his voice. There is something about a real leader that makes it unnecessary for him to get tough.

But back to the survey—I didn't see much of it as I was up to my elbows in pots and pans, but I knew what was going on. The valley we were in had been picked from photographs taken from the *Jitterbug;* it was now up to Paul to decide whether or not it was ideally suited to easy colonization. It had the advantage of being in direct line-of-sight with power station number two, but that was not essential. Line-of-sight power relays could be placed anywhere on the

mountains (no name, as yet) just south of us. Most
of the new villages would have to have power relayed
anyhow. Aside from a safety factor for the heat trap
there was no point in setting up extra power stations
when the whole planet couldn't use the potential of
one mass-conversion plant.

So they got busy—an engineering team working on
drainage and probable annual water resources, topog-
raphers getting a contour, a chemistry-agronomy team
checking on what the various rock formations would
make as soil, and a community architect laying out a
town and farm and rocket port plot. There were several other specialists, too, like the mineralogist, Mr.
Villa, who was doodlebugging the place for ores.

Paul was the "general specialist" who balanced all
the data in his mind, fiddled with his slip stick, stared
off into the sky, and came up with the over all answer.
The over all answer for that valley was "nix"—and
we moved on to the next one on the list, packing the
stuff on our backs.

That was one of the few chances I got to look
around. You see, we had landed at sunrise—about
five o'clock Wednesday morning sunrise was, in that
longitude—and the object was to get as much done as
possible during each light phase. Jupiter light is all
right for working in your own fields, but no good for
surveying strange territory—and here we didn't even
have Jupiter light—just Callisto, every other dark
phase, every twelve-and-half days, to be exact. Con-
sequently we worked straight through light phase, on
pep pills.

Now a man who is on the pills will eat more than
twice as much as a man who is sleeping regularly.
You know, the Eskimos have a saying, "Food is sleep."
I had to produce hot meals every four hours, around
the clock. I had no time for sightseeing.

We got to camp number two, pitched our tents, I
served a scratch meal, and Paul passed out sleeping

pills. By then the Sun was down and we really died for about twenty hours. We were comfortable enough —spun glass pads under us and resin sealed glass canvas over us.

I fed them again, Paul passed out more sleepy pills, and back we went to sleep. Paul woke me Monday afternoon. This time I fixed them a light breakfast, then really spread myself to turn them out a feast. Everybody was well rested by now, and not disposed to want to go right back to bed. So I stuffed them.

After that we sat around for a few hours and talked. I got out my squeeze box—brought along by popular demand, that is to say, Paul suggested it—and gave 'em a few tunes. Then we talked some more.

They got to arguing about where life started and somebody brought up the old theory that the Sun had once been much brighter—Jock Montague, it was, the chemist. "Mark my words," he said, "When we get around to exploring Pluto, you'll find that life was there before us. Life is persistent, like mass-energy."

"Nuts," answered Mr. Villa, very politely. "Pluto isn't even a proper planet; it used to be a satellite of Neptune."

"Well, Neptune, then," Jock persisted. "Life is all through the universe. Mark my words—when the Jove Project straightens out the bugs and gets going, they'll even find life on the surface of Jupiter."

"On Jupiter?" Mr. Villa exploded. "Please, Jock! Methane and ammonia and cold as a mother-in-law's kiss. Don't joke with us. Why, there's not even light down under on the surface of Jupiter; it's pitch dark."

"I said it and I'll say it again," Montague answered. "Life is persistent. Wherever there is mass and energy with conditions that permit the formation of large and stable molecules, there you will find life. Look at Mars. Look at Venus. Look at Earth—the most dangerous planet of the lot. Look at the Ruined Planet."

I said, "What do you think about it, Paul?"

The boss smiled gently. "I don't. I haven't enough data."

"There!" said Mr. Villa. "There speaks a wise man. Tell me, Jock, how did you get to be an authority on this subject?"

"I have the advantage," Jock answered grandly, "of not knowing too much about the subject. Facts are always a handicap in philosophical debate."

That ended that phase of it, for Mr. Seymour, the boss agronomist, said, "I'm not so much worried about where life came from as where it is going—here."

"How?" I wanted to know. "In what way?"

"What are we going to make of this planet? We can make it anything we want. Mars and Venus—they had native cultures. We dare not change them much and we'll never populate them very heavily. These Jovian moons are another matter; it's up to us. They say man is endlessly adaptable. I say on the contrary that man doesn't adapt himself as much as he adapts his environment. Certainly we are doing so here. But how?"

"I thought that was pretty well worked out," I said. "We set up these new centers, more people come in and we spread out, same as at Leda."

"Ah, but where does it stop? We have three ships making regular trips now. Shortly there will be a ship in every three weeks, then it will be every week, then every day. Unless we are almighty careful there will be food rationing here, same as on Earth. Bill, do you know how fast the population is increasing, back Earthside?"

I admitted that I didn't.

"More than one hundred thousand more persons each day than there were the day before. Figure that up."

I did. "That would be, uh, maybe fifteen, twenty shiploads a day. Still, I imagine they could build ships to carry them."

"Yes, *but where would we put them?* Each day,

more than twice as many people landing as there are now on this whole globe. And not just on Monday, but on Tuesday, and Wednesday, and Thursday—and the week and the month and the year after that, just to keep Earth's population stable. I tell you, it won't work. The day will come when we will have to *stop immigration entirely*." He looked around aggressively, like a man who expects to be contradicted.

He wasn't disappointed. Somebody said, "Oh, Seymour, come off it! Do you think you own this place just because you got here first? You snuck in while the rules were lax."

"You can't argue with mathematics," Seymour insisted. "Ganymede has got to be made self-sufficient as soon as possible—and then we've got to slam the door!"

Paul was shaking his head. "It won't be necessary."

"Huh?" said Seymour. "Why not? Answer me that. You represent the Commission: what fancy answer has the Commission got?"

"None," Paul told him. "And your figures are right but your conclusions are wrong. Oh, Ganymede has to be made self-sufficient, true enough, but your bogeyman about a dozen or more shiploads of immigrants a day you can forget."

"Why, if I may be so bold?"

Paul looked around the tent and grinned apologetically. "Can you stand a short dissertation on population dynamics? I'm afraid I don't have Jock's advantage; this is a subject I am supposed to know something about."

Somebody said, "Stand back. Give him air."

"Okay," Paul went on, "you brought it on yourselves. A lot of people have had the idea that colonization is carried on with the end purpose of relieving the pressure of people and hunger back on Earth. Nothing could be further from the truth."

I said, "Huh?"

"Bear with me. Not only is it physically impossible for a little planet to absorb the increase of a big planet, as Seymour pointed out, but there is another reason why we'll never get any such flood of people as a hundred thousand people a day—a psychological reason. There are never as many people willing to emigrate (even if you didn't pick them over) as there are new people born. Most people simply will not leave home. Most of them won't even leave their native villages, much less go to a far planet."

Mr. Villa nodded. "I go along with you on that. The willing emigrant is an odd breed of cat. He's scarce."

"Right," Paul agreed. "But let's suppose for a moment that a hundred thousand people were willing to emigrate every day and Ganymede and the other colonies could take them. Would that relieve the situation back home—I mean 'back Earthside'? The answer is, 'No, it wouldn't'."

He appeared to have finished. I finally said, "Excuse my blank look, Paul, but why wouldn't it?"

"Studied any bionomics, Bill?"

"Some."

"Mathematical population bionomics?"

"Well—no."

"But you do know that in the greatest wars the Earth ever had there were always more people after the war than before, no matter how many were killed. Life is not merely persistent, as Jock puts it; life is explosive. The basic theorem of population mathematics *to which there has never been found an exception* is that population increases always, not merely up to extent of the food supply, but beyond it, to the minimum diet that will sustain life—the ragged edge of starvation. In other words, if we bled off a hundred thousand people a day, the Earth's population would then grow until the increase was around *two* hundred thousand a day, or the bionomical maximum for Earth's new ecological dynamic."

Nobody said anything for a moment; there wasn't anything to say. Presently Sergei spoke up with, "You paint a grim picture, boss. What's the answer?"

Paul said, "There isn't any!"

Sergei said, "I didn't mean it that way. I mean, what is the outcome?"

When Paul did answer it was just one word, one monosyllable, spoken so softly that it would not have been heard if there had not been dead silence. What he said was:

"War."

There was a shuffle and a stir; it was an unthinkable idea. Seymour said, "Come now, Mr. du Maurier—I may be a pessimist, but I'm not that much of one. Wars are no longer possible."

Paul said, "So?"

Seymour answered almost belligerently, "Are you trying to suggest that the Space Patrol would let us down? Because that is the only way a war could happen."

Paul shook his head. "The Patrol won't let us down. But they won't be able to stop it. A police force is all right for stopping individual disturbances; it's fine for nipping things in the bud. But when the disturbances are planet wide, no police force is big enough, or strong enough, or wise enough. They'll try—they'll try bravely. They won't succeed."

"You really believe that?"

"It's my considered opinion. And not only my opinion, but the opinion of the Commission. Oh, I don't mean the political board; I mean the career scientists."

"Then what in tarnation is the Commission up to?"

"Building colonies. We think that is worthwhile in itself. The colonies need not be affected by the War. In fact, I don't think they will be, not much. It will be like America was up to the end of the nineteenth century; European troubles passed her by. I rather expect that the War, when it comes, will be of such size and duration that interplanetary travel will cease to be for a considerable period. That is why I said this planet has got to be self-sufficient. It takes a high technical culture to maintain interplanetary travel and Earth may not have it—after a bit."

I think Paul's ideas were a surprise to everyone present; I know they were to me. Seymour jabbed a finger at him, "If you believe this, then why are you going back to Earth? Tell me that."

Again Paul spoke softly. "I'm not. I'm going to stay here and become a 'steader."

Suddenly I knew why he was letting his beard grow.

Seymour answered, "Then you expect it soon." It was not a question; it was a statement.

"Having gone this far," Paul said hesitantly, "I'll give you a direct answer. War is not less than forty Earth years away, not more than seventy."

You could feel a sigh of relief all around the place. Seymour continued to speak for us, "Forty to seventy, you say. But that's no reason to homestead; you probably wouldn't live to see it. Not but what you'd make a good neighbor."

"I see this War," Paul insisted. "I know it's coming. Should I leave it up to my hypothetical children and grandchildren to outguess it? No. Here I rest. If I marry, I'll marry here. I'm not raising any kids to be radioactive dust."

It must have been about here that Hank stuck his head in the tent, for I don't remember anyone answering Paul. Hank had been outside on business of his own; now he opened the flap and called out, "Hey gents! Europa is up!"

We all trooped out to see. We went partly through embarrassment, I think; Paul had been too nakedly honest. But we probably would have gone anyhow. Sure, we saw Europa every day of our lives at home, but not the way we were seeing it now.

Since Europa goes around Jupiter inside Ganymede's

orbit, it never gets very far away from Jupiter, if you call 39 degrees "not very far." Since we were 113 west longitude, Jupiter was 23 degrees below our eastern horizon—which meant that Europa, when it was furthest west of Jupiter, would be a maximum of 16 degrees above the true horizon.

Excuse the arithmetic. Since we had a row of high hills practically sitting on us to the east, what all this means is that, once a week, Europa would rise above the hills, just peeking over, hang there for about a day—then turn around and set in the east, right where it had risen. Up and down like an elevator.

If you've never been off Earth, don't tell me it's impossible. That's how it is—Jupiter and its moons do some funny things.

It was the first time it had happened this trip, so we watched it—a little silver boat, riding the hills like waves, with its horns turned up. There was argument about whether or not it was still rising, or starting to set again, and much comparing of watches. Some claimed to be able to detect motion but they weren't agreed on which way. After a while I got cold and went back in.

But I was glad of the interruption. I had a feeling that Paul had said considerably more than he had intended to and more than he would be happy to recall, come light phase. I blamed it on the sleeping pills. Sleeping pills are all right when necessary, but they tend to make you babble and tell your right name—treacherous things.

19. The Other People

By the end of the second light phase it was clear—
to Paul, anyhow—that this second valley would do.
It wasn't the perfect valley and maybe there was a
better one just over the ridge—but life is too short.
Paul assigned it a score of 92% by some complicated
system thought up by the Commission, which was
seven points higher than passing. The perfect valley
could wait for the colonials to find it . . . which they
would, some day.

We named the valley Happy Valley, just for luck,
and named the mountains south of it the Pauline
Peaks, over Paul's protests. He said it wasn't official
anyway; we said we would see to it that it was made
so—and the boss topographer, Abie Finkelstein, marked
it so on the map and we all intialed it.

We spent the third light phase rounding up the de-
tails. We could have gone back then, if there had been
any way to get back. There wasn't, so we had to dope
through another dark phase. Some of them preferred
to go back on a more normal schedule instead; there
was a round-the-clock poker game, which I stayed out
of, having nothing I could afford to lose and no talent
for filling straights. There were more dark phase bull
sessions but they never got as grave as the first one

and nobody ever again asked Paul what he thought about the future prospects of things.

By the end of the third dark phase I was getting more than a little tired of seeing nothing but the inside of our portable range. I asked Paul for some time off.

Hank had been helping me since the start of the third dark phase. He had been working as a topographical assistant; flash contour pictures were on the program at the start of that dark phase. He was supposed to get an open-lens shot across the valley from an elevation on the south just as a sunburst flash was let off from an elevation to the west.

Hank had a camera of his own, just acquired, and he was shutter happy, always pointing it at things. This time he had tried to get a picture of his own as well as the official picture. He had goofed off, missed the official picture entirely, and to top it off had failed to protect his eyes when the sunburst went off. Which put him on the sick list and I got him as kitchen police.

He was all right shortly, but Finkelstein didn't want him back. So I asked for relief for both of us, so we could take a hike together and do a little exploring. Paul let us go.

There had been high excitement at the end of the second light phase when lichen had been discovered near the west end of the valley. For a while it looked as if native life had been found on Ganymede. It was a false alarm—careful examination showed that it was not only an Earth type, but a type authorized by the bionomics board.

But it did show one thing—life was spreading, taking hold, at a point thirty-one hundred miles from the original invasion. There was much argument as to whether the spores had been air borne, or had been brought in on the clothing of the crew who had set up the power plant. It didn't matter, really.

But Hank and I decided to explore off that way and

see if we could find more of it. Besides it was away from the way we had come from camp number one. We didn't tell Paul we were going after lichen because we were afraid he would veto it; the stuff had been found quite some distance from camp. He had warned us not to go too far and to be back by six o'clock Thursday morning, in time to break camp and head back to our landing point, where the *Jitterbug* was to meet us.

I agreed as I didn't mean to go far in any case. I didn't much care whether we found lichen or not; I wasn't feeling well. But I kept that fact to myself; I wasn't going to be done out of my one and only chance to see some of the country.

We didn't find any more lichen. We did find the crystals.

We were trudging along, me as happy as a kid let out of school despite an ache in my side and Hank taking useless photographs of odd rocks and lava flows. Hank had been saying that he thought he would sell out his place and homestead here in Happy Valley. He said, "You know, Bill, they are going to need a few real Ganymede farmers here to give the greenhorns the straight dope. And who knows more about Ganymede-style farming than I do?"

"Almost everybody," I assured him.

He ignored it. "This place has really got it," he went on, gazing around at a stretch of country that looked like Armageddon after a hard battle. "Much better than around Leda."

I admitted that it had possibilities. "But I don't think it's for me," I went on. "I don't think I'd care to settle anywhere where you can't see Jupiter."

"Nonsense!" he answered. "Did you come here to stare at the sights or to make a farm?"

"That's a moot point," I admitted. "Sometimes I think one thing, sometimes the other. Sometimes I don't have the foggiest idea."

He wasn't listening. "See that slot up there?"

"Sure. What about it?"

"If we crossed that little glacier, we could get up to it."

"Why?"

"I think it leads into another valley—which might be even better. Nobody has been up there. I know—I was in the topo gang."

"I've been trying to help you forget that," I told him. "But why look at all? There must be a hundred thousand valleys on Ganymede that nobody has looked at. Are you in the real estate business?" It didn't appeal to me. There is something that gets you about virgin soil on Ganymede; I wanted to stay in sight of camp. It was quiet as a library—quieter. On Earth there is always some sound, even in the desert. After a while the stillness and the bare rocks and the ice and the craters get on my nerves.

"Come on! Don't be a sissy!" he answered, and started climbing.

The slot did not lead to another valley; it led into a sort of corridor in the hills. One wall was curiously flat, as if it had been built that way on purpose. We went along it a way, and I was ready to turn back and had stopped to call to Hank, who had climbed the loose rock on the other side to get a picture. As I turned, my eye caught some color and I moved up to see what it was. It was the crystals.

I stared at them and they seemed to stare back. I called, "Hey! Hank! Come here on the bounce!"

"What's up?"

"Come here! Here's something worth taking a picture of."

He scrambled down and joined me. After a bit he let out his breath and whispered, "Well, I'll be fried on Friday!"

Hank got busy with his camera. I never saw such crystals, not even stalactites in caves. They were six-sided, except a few that were three-sided and some that were twelve-sided. They came anywhere from little squatty fellows no bigger than a button mushroom up to tall, slender stalks, knee high. Later on and further up we found some chest high.

They were not simple prisms; they branched and budded. But the thing that got you was the colors.

They were all colors and they changed color as you looked at them. We finally decided that they didn't have any color at all; it was just refraction of light. At least Hank thought so.

He shot a full cartridge of pictures then said, "Come on. Let's see where they come from."

I didn't want to. I was shaky from the climb and my right side was giving me fits every step I took. I guess I was dizzy, too; when I looked at the crystals they seemed to writhe around and I would have to blink my eyes to steady them.

But Hank had already started so I followed. The crystals seemed to keep to what would have been the water bed of the canyon, had it been spring. They seemed to need water. We came to a place where there was a drift of ice across the floor of the corridor —ancient ice, with a thin layer of last winter's snow on top of it. The crystals had carved a passage right through it, a natural bridge of ice, and had cleared a space of several feet on each side of where they were growing, as well.

Hank lost his footing as we scrambled through and snatched at one of the crystals. It broke off with a sharp, clear note, like a silver bell.

Hank straightened up and stood looking at his hand. There were parallel cuts across his palm and fingers. He stared at them stupidly.

"That'll teach you," I said, and then got out a first-aid kit and bandaged it for him. When I had finished I said, "Now let's go back."

"Shucks," he said. "What's a few little cuts? Come on."

I said, "Look, Hank, I want to go back. I don't feel good."

"What's the matter?"

"Stomach ache."

"You eat too much; that's your trouble. The exercise will do you good."

"No, Hank. I've got to go back."

He stared up the ravine and looked fretful. Finally he said, "Bill, I think I see where the crystals come from, not very far up. You wait here and let me take a look. Then I'll come back and we'll head for camp. I won't be gone long; honest I won't."

"Okay," I agreed. He started up; shortly I followed him. I had had it pounded into my head as a Cub not to get separated in a strange country.

After a bit I heard him shout. I looked up and saw him standing, facing a great dark hole in the cliff. I called out, "What's the matter?"

He answered:

"GREAT JUMPING HOLY SMOKE!!!"—like that.

"What's the matter?" I repeated irritably and hurried along until I was standing beside him.

The crystals continued up the place where we were. They came right to the cave mouth, but did not go in; they formed a solid dense thicket across the threshold. Lying across the floor of the ravine, as if it had been tumbled there by an upheaval like the big quake, was a flat rock, a monolith, Stonehenge size. You could see where it had broken off the cliff, uncovering the hole. The plane of cleavage was as sharp and smooth as anything done by the ancient Egyptians.

But that wasn't what we were looking at; we were looking into the hole.

It was dark inside, but diffused light, reflected off the canyon floor and the far wall, filtered inside. My eyes began to adjust and I could see what Hank was staring at, what he had exploded about.

There were *things* in there and they weren't natural.

I couldn't have told you what sort of things because they were like nothing I had ever seen before in my life, or seen pictures of—or heard of. How can you describe what you've never seen before and have no words for? Shucks, you can't even *see* a thing properly the first time you see it; your eye doesn't take in the pattern.

But I could see this: they weren't rocks, they weren't plants, they weren't animals. They were *made* things, man made—well, maybe not "man" made, but not things that just happen, either.

I wanted very badly to get up close to them and see what they were. For the moment, I forgot I was sick.

So did Hank. As usual he said, "Come on! Let's go!"

But I said, "How?"

"Why, we just—" He stopped and took another look. "Well, let's see, we go around— No. Hmm . . . Bill, we will have to bust up some of those crystals and go right through the middle. There's no other way to get in."

I said, "Isn't one chopped up hand enough for you?"

"I'll bust 'em with a rock. It seems a shame; they are so pretty, but that's what I'll have to do."

"I don't think you can bust those big ones. Besides that, I'll give you two to one that they are sharp enough to cut through your boots."

"I'll chance it." He found a chunk of rock and made an experiment; I was right on both counts. Hank stopped and looked the situation over, whistling softly. "Bill——"

"Yeah?"

"See that little ledge over the opening?"

"What about it?"

"It comes out to the left further than the crystals do. I'm going to pile rock up high enough for us to reach it, then we can go along it and drop down right in front of the cave mouth. The crystals don't come that close."

I looked it over and decided it would work. "But how do we get back?"

"We can pile up some of that stuff we can see inside and shinny up again. At the very worst I can boost you up on my shoulders and then you can reach down your belt to me, or something."

If I had my wits about me, maybe I would have protested. But we tried it and it worked—worked right up to the point where I was hanging by my fingers from the ledge over the cave mouth.

I felt a stabbing pain in my side and let go.

I came to with Hank shaking me. "Let me alone!" I growled.

"You knocked yourself out," he said. "I didn't know you were so clumsy." I didn't answer. I just gathered my knees up to my stomach and closed my eyes.

Hank shook me again. "Don't you want to see what's in here?"

I kicked at him. "I don't want to see the Queen of Sheba! Can't you see I'm sick?" I closed my eyes again.

I must have passed out. When I woke up, Hank was sitting Turk fashion in front of me, with my torch in his hand. "You've been asleep a long time, fellow," he said gently. "Feel any better?"

"Not much."

"Try to pull yourself together and come along with me. You've got to see this, Bill. You won't believe it. This is the greatest discovery since—well, since— Never mind; Columbus was a piker. We're famous, Bill."

"You may be famous," I said. "I'm sick."

"Where does it hurt?"

"All over. My stomach is hard as a rock—a rock with a toothache."

"Bill," he said seriously, "have you ever had your appendix out?"

"No."

"Hmmm . . . maybe you should have had it out."

"Well, this is a fine time to tell me!"

"Take it easy."

"Take it easy, my foot!" I got up on one elbow, my head swimming. "Hank, listen to me. You've got to get back to camp and tell them. Have them send a tractor for me."

"Look, Bill," he said gently, "you know there isn't anything like a tractor at camp."

I tried to struggle with the problem but it was too much for me. My brain was fuzzy. "Well, have them bring a stretcher, at least," I said peevishly and lay down again.

Some time later I felt him fumbling around with my clothes. I tried to push him away, then I felt something very cold on me. I took a wild swing at him; it didn't connect.

"Steady," he said. "I have found some ice. Don't squirm around or you'll knock off the pack."

"I don't want it."

"You've got to have it. You keep that ice pack in place until we get out of here and you may live to be hanged, yet."

I was too feeble to resist. I lay back down and closed my eyes again. When I opened my eyes again, I was amazed to feel better. Instead of feeling ready to die, I merely felt awful. Hank wasn't around; I called to him. When he didn't answer at once I felt panicky.

Then he came trotting up, waving the torch. "I thought you had gone," I said.

"No. To tell the truth, I can't get out of here. I can't get back up to the ledge and I can't get over the crystals. I tried it." He held up one boot; it was in shreds and there was blood on it.

"Hurt yourself?"

"I'll live."

"I wonder," I answered. "Nobody knows we are here—and you say we can't get out. Looks like we starve. Not that I give a hoot."

'Speaking of that," he said. "I saved you some of our

lunch. I'm afraid I didn't leave much; you were asleep a long, long time."

"Don't mention food!" I retched and grabbed at my side.

"Sorry. But look—I didn't say we couldn't get out."

"But you did."

"No, I said *I* couldn't get out."

"What's the difference?"

"Uh, never mind. But I think we'll get out. It was what you said about getting a tractor——"

"Tractor? Are you out of your head?"

"Skip it," Bill answered. "There is a sort of tractor thing back there—or more like a scaffolding, maybe."

"Make up your mind."

"Call it a wagon. I think I can get it out, at least across the crystals. We could use it as a bridge."

"Well, roll it out."

"It doesn't roll. It, uh—well, it walks."

I tried to get up. "This I got to see."

"Just move over out of the way of the door."

I managed to get to my feet, with Hank helping me. "I'm coming along."

"Want the ice pack changed?"

"Later, maybe." Hank took me back and showed me. I don't know how to describe the walker wagon—maybe you've seen pictures since. If a centipede were a dinosaur and made of metal to boot, it would be a walker wagon. The body of it was a sort of trough and it was supported by thirty-eight legs, nineteen on a side.

"That," I said, "is the craziest contraption I ever laid eyes on. You'll never shove it out the door."

"Wait until you see," he advised. "And if you think this is crazy, you should see the other things in here."

"Such as?"

"Bill, you know what I think this place is? I think it's a hangar for a space ship."

"Huh? Don't be silly; space ships don't have hangars."

"This one has."

"You mean you *saw* a space ship in here?"

"Well, I don't know. It's not like any I ever saw before, but if it's not a space ship, I don't know what it is good for."

I wanted to go see, but Hank objected. "Another time, Bill; we've got to get back to camp. We're late as it is."

I didn't put up any fight. My side was paining me again, from the walk. "Okay, what happens next?"

"Like this." He led me around to the end of the contraption; the trough came nearly down to the floor in back. Hank helped me get inside, told me to lie down, and went up to the other end. "The guy that built this," he said, "must have been a hump-backed midget with four arms. Hang on."

"Do you know what you're doing?" I asked.

"I moved it about six feet before; then I lost my nerve. Abracadabra! Hold onto your hat!" He poked a finger deep into a hole.

The thing began to move, silently, gently, without any fuss. When we came out into the sunshine, Hank pulled his finger out of the hole. I sat up. The thing was two thirds out of the cave and the front end was beyond the crystals.

I sighed. "You made it, Hank, Let's get going. If I had some more ice on my side I think I could walk."

"Wait a second," he said. "I want to try something. There are holes here I haven't stuck a finger in yet."

"Leave well enough alone."

Instead of answering he tried another hole. The machine backed up suddenly. "Woops!" he said, jerked his finger out, and jabbed it back where it had been before. He left it there until he regained what we had lost.

He tried other holes more cautiously. At last he found one which caused the machine to rear up its front end slightly and swing it to the left, like a caterpillar. "Now we are in business," he said happily. "I can steer it." We started down the canyon.

Hank was not entirely correct in thinking he could guide it. It was more like guiding a horse than a machine—or perhaps more like guiding one of those new groundmobiles with the semi-automatic steering. The walker wagon came to the little natural bridge of ice through which the crystals passed and stopped of itself. Hank tried to get it to go through the opening, which was large enough; it would have none of it. The front end cast around like a dog sniffing, then eased gradually up hill and around the ice.

It stayed level; apparently it could adjust its legs, like the fabulous hillside snee.

When Hank came to the ice flow we had crossed on the way up to the notch, he stopped it and gave me a fresh ice pack. Apparently it did not object to ice in itself, but simply refused to go through holes, for when we started up again, it crossed the little glacier, slowly and cautiously, but steadily.

We headed on toward camp. "This," Hank announced happily, "is the greatest cross-country, rough-terrain vehicle ever built. I wish I knew what makes it go. If I had the patent on this thing, I'd be rich."

"It's yours; you found it."

"It doesn't really belong to me."

"Hank," I answered, "you don't really think the owner is going to come back looking for it, do you?"

He got a very odd look. "No, I don't, Bill. Say, Bill, uh, how long ago do you think this thing was put in there?"

"I wouldn't even want to guess."

There was only one tent at the camp site. As we came up to it, somebody came out and waited for us. It was Sergei.

"Where have you guys been?" he asked. "And where in Kingdom Come did you steal *that?*

"And what *is* it?" he added.

We did our best to bring him up to date, and presently he did the same for us. They had searched for us as long as they could, then Paul had been forced to move back to camp number one to keep the date with the *Jitterbug*. He had left Sergei behind to fetch us when we showed up. "He left a note for you," Sergei added, digging it out.

It read:

> "*Dear Pen Pals,*
>
> "*I am sorry to go off and leave you crazy galoots but you know the schedule as well as I do. I would stay behind myself to herd you home, but your pal Sergei insists that it is his privilege. Every time I try to reason with him he crawls further back into his hole, bares his teeth, and growls.*
>
> "*As soon as you get this, get your chubby little legs to moving in the direction of camp number one. Run, do not walk. We'll hold the Jitterbug, but you know how dear old Aunt Hattie feels about keeping her schedule. She isn't going to like it if you are late.*
>
> "*When I see you, I intend to beat your ears down around your shoulders.*
>
> "*Good luck,*
> "*P. du M.*
> "*P.S. to Doctor Slop: I took care of your accordion.*"

When we had finished reading it Sergei said, "I want to hear more about what you found—about eight times more. But not now; we've got to tear over to camp number one. Hank, you think Bill can't walk it?"

I answered for myself, an emphatic "no." The excitement was wearing off and I was feeling worse again.

"Hmm—Hank, do you think that mobile junk yard will carry us over there?"

"I think it will carry us any place." Hank patted it.

"How fast? The *Jitterbug* has already grounded."

"Are you sure?" asked Hank.

"I saw its trail in the sky at least three hours ago."

"Let's get going!"

I don't remember much about the trip. They stopped once in the pass, and packed me with ice again. The next thing I knew I was awakened by hearing Sergei shout, "There's the *Jitterbug!* I can see it."

"*Jitterbug*, here we come," answered Hank. I sat up and looked, too.

We were coming down the slope, not five miles from it, when flame burst from its tail and it climbed for the sky.

Hank groaned. I lay back down and closed my eyes.

I woke up again when the contraption stopped. Paul was there, hands on his hips, staring at us. "About time you birds got home," he announced. "But where did you find *that?*"

"Paul," Hank said urgently, "Bill is very sick."

"Oh, oh!" Paul swung up and into the walker and made no more questions then. A moment later he had my belly bared and was shoving a thumb into that spot between the belly button and the hip bone. "Does that hurt?" he asked.

I was too weak to slug him. He gave me a pill.

I took no further part in events for a while, but what had happened was this: Captain Hattie had waited, at Paul's urgent insistence, for a couple of hours, and then had announced that she had to blast. She had a schedule to keep with the *Covered Wagon* and she had no intention, she said, of keeping eight thousand people waiting for the benefit of two. Hank and I could play Indian if we liked; we couldn't play hob with her schedule.

There was nothing Paul could do, so he sent the rest back and waited for us.

But I didn't hear this at the time. I was vaguely aware that we were in the walker wagon, travelling, and I woke up twice when I was repacked with ice, but the whole episode is foggy. They travelled east, with Hank driving and Paul navigating—by the seat of his pants. Some long dreamy time later they reached a pioneer camp surveying a site over a hundred miles away—and from there Paul radioed for help.

Whereupon the *Jitterbug* came and got us. I remember the landing back at Leda—that is, I remember somebody saying, "Hurry, there! We've got a boy with a burst appendix."

20. Home

There was considerable excitement over what we had found—and there still is—but I didn't see any of it. I was busy playing games with the Pearly Gates. I guess I have Dr. Archibald to thank for still being here. And Hank. And Sergei. And Paul. And Captain Hattie. And some nameless party, who lived somewhere, a long time ago, whose shape and race I still don't know, but who designed the perfect machine for traveling overland through rough country.

I thanked everybody but him. They all came to see me in the hospital, even Captain Hattie, who growled at me, then leaned over and kissed me on the cheek as she left. I was so surprised I almost bit her.

The Schultzes came, of course, and Mama cried over me and Papa gave me an apple and Gretchen could hardly talk, which isn't like her. And Molly brought the twins down to see me and vice versa.

The Leda daily *Planet* interviewed me. They wanted to know whether or not we thought the things we found were made by men?

Now that is a hard question to answer and smarter people than myself have worked on it since.

What is a man?

The things Hank and I—and the Project Jove scientists who went later—found in that cave couldn't have been made by men—not men like us. The walker wagon was the simplest thing they found. Most of the things they still haven't found out the use for. Nor have they figured out what the creatures looked like—no pictures.

That seems surprising, but the scientists concluded they didn't have eyes—not eyes like ours, anyhow. So they didn't use pictures.

The very notion of a "picture" seems pretty esoteric when you think it over. The Venerians don't use pictures, nor the Martians. Maybe we are the only race in the universe that thought up that way of recording things.

So they weren't "men"—not like us.

But they *were* men in the real sense of the word, even though I don't doubt that I would run screaming away if I met one in a dark alley. The important thing, as Mr. Seymour would say, they had—they controlled their environment. They weren't animals, pushed around and forced to accept what nature handed them; they took nature and bent it to their will.

I guess they were men.

The crystals were one of the oddest things about it and I didn't have any opinions on that. Somehow, those crystals were connected with that cave—or space ship hangar, or whatever it was. Yet they couldn't or wouldn't go inside the cave.

Here was another point that the follow-up party from Project Jove recorded: that big unwieldly walker wagon came all the way down that narrow canyon— yet it did not step on a single crystal. Hank must be a pretty good driver. He says he's not that good.

Don't ask me. I don't understand everything that goes on in the universe. It's a big place.

I had lots of time to think before they let me out of

the hospital—and lots to think about. I thought about my coming trip to Earth, to go back to school. I had missed the *Covered Wagon*, of course, but that didn't mean anything; I could take the *Mayflower* three weeks later. But did I want to go? It was a close thing to decide.

One thing I was sure of: I was going to take those merit badge tests as soon as I was out of bed. I had put it off too long. A close brush with the hereafter reminds you that you don't have forever to get things done.

But going back to school? That was another matter. For one thing, as Dad told me, the council had lost its suit with the Commission; Dad couldn't use his Earthside assets.

And there was the matter that Paul had talked about the night he had to let his hair down—the coming war.

Did Paul know what he was talking about? If so, was I letting it scare me out? I honestly didn't think so; Paul had said that it was not less than forty years away. I wouldn't be Earthside more than four or five years—and, besides, how could you get scared of anything that far in the future?

I had been through the Quake and the reconstruction; I didn't really think I'd ever be scared of anything again.

I had a private suspicion that, supposing there was a war, I'd go join up; I wouldn't be running away from it. Silly, maybe.

No, I wasn't afraid of the War, but it was on my mind. Why? I finally doped it out. When Paul called I asked him about it. "See here, Paul—this war you were talking about: when Ganymede reaches the state that Earth has gotten into, does that mean war here, too? Not now—a few centuries from now."

He smiled rather sadly. "By then we may know enough to keep from getting into that shape. At least we can hope."

He got a far-away look and added, "A new colony is always a new hope."

I liked that way of putting it. "A new hope—" Once I heard somebody call a new baby that.

I still didn't have the answer about going back when Dad called on me one Sunday night. I put it up to him about the cost of the fare. "I know the land is technically mine, George—but it's too much of a drain on you two."

"Contrariwise," said George, "we'll get by and that's what savings are for. Molly is for it. We will be sending the twins back for school, you know."

"Even so, I don't feel right about it. And what real use is there in it, George? I don't need a fancy education. I've been thinking about Callisto: there's a brand new planet not touched yet with great opportunities for a man in on the ground floor. I could get a job with the atmosphere expedition—Paul would put in a word for me—and grow up with the project. I might be chief engineer of the whole planet some day."

"Not unless you learn more about thermodynamics than you do now, you won't be!"

"Huh?"

"Engineers don't just 'grow up'; they study. They go to school."

"Don't I study? Ain't I attending two of your classes right now? I can get to be an engineer here; I don't have to drag back half a billion miles for it."

"Fiddlesticks! It takes discipline to study. You haven't even taken your merit badge tests. You've let your Eagle Scoutship lapse."

I wanted to explain that taking tests and studying for tests were two different things—that I *had* studied. But I couldn't seem to phrase it right.

George stood up. "See here, Son, I'm going to put it to you straight. Never mind about being chief engineer of a planet; these days even a farmer needs the

best education he can get. Without it he's just a
country bumpkin, a stumbling peasant, poking seeds
into the ground and hoping a miracle will make
them grow. I want you to go back to Earth and get the
best that Earth has to offer. I want you to have a
degree with prestige behind it—M.I.T., Harvard, the
Sorbonne. Some place noted for scholarship. Take the
time to do that and then do anything you want to do.
Believe me, it will pay."

I thought about it and answered, "I guess you are
right, George."

Dad stood up. "Well, make up your mind. I'll have
to hurry now for the bus, or I'll be hoofing it back to
the farm. See you tomorrow."

"Good night, George."

I lay awake and thought about it. After a while,
Mrs. Dinsmore, the wing nurse, came in, turned out
my light, and said goodnight. But I didn't go to sleep.

Dad was right, I knew. I didn't want to be an
ignoramus. Furthermore, I had seen the advantage
held by men with fancy degrees—first crack at the
jobs, fast promotion. Okay, I'd get me one of those
sheepskins, then come back and—well, go to Callisto,
maybe, or perhaps prove a new parcel of land. I'd
go and I'd come back.

Nevertheless I couldn't get to sleep. After a while
I glanced at my new watch and saw that it was nearly
midnight—dawn in a few minutes. I decided that I
wanted to see it. It might be the last time I'd be up
and around at midnight Sunday for a long, long
time.

I scouted the corridor; Old Lady Dinsmore wasn't
in sight. I ducked outside.

The Sun was just barely below the horizon; north
of me I could see its first rays touching the topmost
antenna of the power station, miles away on Pride
Peak. It was very still and very beautiful. Overhead
old Jupiter was in half phase, bulging and orange and

grand. To the west of it Io was just coming out of shadow; it passed from black to cherry red to orange as I watched.

I wondered how I would feel to be back on Earth? How would it feel to weigh three times as much as I did now? I didn't feel heavy; I felt just right.

How would it feel to swim in that thick dirty soup they use for air?

How would it feel to have nobody but ground hogs to talk to? How could I talk to a girl who wasn't a colonial, who had never been off Earth higher than a copter hop? Sissies. Take Gretchen, now—there was a girl who could kill a chicken and have it in the pot while an Earthside girl would still be squealing.

The top of the Sun broke above the horizon and caught the snow on the peaks of the Big Rock Candy Mountains, tinting it rosy against a pale green sky. I began to be able to see the country around me. It was a new, hard, clean place—not like California with its fifty, sixty million people falling over each other. It was my kind of a place—it was *my* place.

The deuce with Caltech and Cambridge and those fancy schools! I'd show Dad it didn't take ivied halls to get an education. Yes, and I'd pass those tests and be an Eagle again, first thing.

Hadn't Andrew Johnson, that American President, learned to read while he was working? Even after he was married? Give us time; we'd have as good scientists and scholars here as anywhere.

The long slow dawn went on and the light caught Kneiper's cut west of me, outlining it. I was reminded of the night we had struggled through it in the storm. As Hank put it, there was one good thing about colonial life—it sorted out the men from the boys.

"I have lived and worked with men." The phrase rang through my head. Rhysling? Kipling, maybe. I had lived and worked with men!

The Sun was beginning to reach the roof tops. It spread across Laguna Serenidad, turning it from black to purple to blue. This was my planet, this was my home and I knew that I would never leave it.

Mrs. Dinsmore came bustling out to the door and spotted me. "Why, the very idea!" she scolded. "You get back where you belong!"

I smiled at her. "I am where I belong. And I'm going to stay!"

ROBERT A. HEINLEIN